I0546013

Other books by Sandra Barret . . .

Terran-Novan Universe Series

Book 1
Face of the Enemy

In Keisha's Shadow
Lavender Secrets

TERRAN-NOVAN UNIVERSE BOOK 2

BLOOD OF A TRAITOR

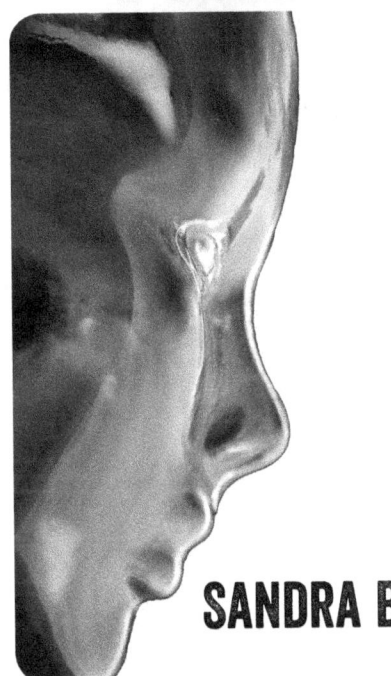

SANDRA BARRET

Mindancer
Bedazzled Ink Publishing Company * Fairfield, California

978-1-939562-32-6 paperback
978-1-939562-33-3 ebook

Cover Design
by
TreeHouse Studio

Mindancer Press
a division of
Bedazzled Ink Publishing Company
Fairfield, California
http://www.bedazzledink.com/

For Ma, who raised us all to know better,
even if we don't act it sometimes.

CHAPTER 1

"Private First Class Kay Deetchu, prep them on the details of the mission." Corporal Jax waved Kay forward and stepped down from the podium.

Kay took his place on the podium and flicked on the vid. The Chun asteroid belt displayed behind her with an overlay of the mining colonies their squads were liberating from the Terrans. "These are the four main asteroids—Yuan, Yin, Tan, and Xi."

She switched the vid to show the Novan mining camp on the fourth asteroid. "Second squad is combining with the Third and Fourth fire team to secure the processing plant on Xi. We drop ship in, and Fourth fire team blows a hole for us in this gray blob. The original mining company specs say this opens into a maintenance tunnel. Fourth fire team stays there to protect our exit while the rest of us secure the facility section by section."

Kay flicked off the vid. "The Terrans have had three months to revamp the defenses they blew away when they captured the mining colonies, but Novan Intel doesn't think they've modified much."

Kay paused to let the grumbling settle down. No one trusted Intel, at least no one who wanted to live through their next mission. She didn't join the grumbling, for Jax's sake.

"The *Kasai* will maneuver close enough to our designated target to drop ship us in, and then it will back off and let the rest of the big-gun warships in the convoy take over close range offensive positions. It's standard-issue bio suits and station-safe munitions only once we're inside the plant."

Kay left the platform. "Suit up and be on your assigned drop ship in twenty minutes."

"Dismissed," Jax said.

The rest of the Marines filed out as he stood by the hatch to give each squad member a nod or a pat on the back, as if his newbie squad leader role wasn't obvious enough.

Kay was the last one out. "Pat my back, and you'll lead your first mission with a broken arm."

"You think I was too friendly?" he asked as he pulled the mission-room hatch shut behind them.

"No, just the right amount of 'You're about to get your ass blown off' friendly. You're a two-meter bundle of red, Tarquin-mongrel nerves." Four years of watching each other's backs didn't mean she was going to coddle him on his first lead mission.

Jax ignored her gibe and led the way down the narrow passageway aft toward midship. The *Kasai* wasn't a big ship, not for the Nassien Military Corporation, but it had the usual buzz of pre-mission preparation. Black boots pounded along on the composite deck plates as blue-suited navy personnel rushed past them, and Marines from other squads filed in their same general direction. The ship intercom bellowed commands and mission status that added to the grating noise level. They walked down three passageways on two decks before they reached their quarters. The ship and all personnel, Navy and Marine, belonged to Nassien Military, but the hatch to their quarters was marked by the distinct grey star and crescent over a red planet backdrop that signified the 28th Marine Regiment.

Jax pulled open the hatch. The chatter of fourteen Marines, the combined Second and Third Squads, accosted them as they entered. Tight bunks stacked three levels high, the space between each packed with uniform lockers and mission-gear lockers.

Kay went to her bunk and flipped open her gear locker. She stripped down to tan shorts and tank top. She faced her drab brown bio suit and started the process of suiting up. The tight-fitting suit was tailored to her exact proportions to ensure constant pressurization in the brief time they would be exposed on the asteroid's surface. That meant it was a bitch to pull on, as attested by the random grunts and curses around her as her squad mates suited up.

Ten minutes of fighting her way into the suit and then the boots, and she was nearly ready to go. She pulled out a gray Terran flak vest from her locker and slipped it over her bio suit. It was an awkward fit, but the vest would stop station-save bullets, and not even the Terrans would be stupid enough to stock anything else inside the mine processing plant. She and Jax scavenged the vests off two Terran corpses on their last mission. Not exactly by the book, but their commanding officer didn't punish ingenuity.

Jax struggled harder with his vest. "I'm not ready for this."

She holstered her knife and pistol, then tightened the flak vest straps for him and slipped his oxygen tank into place. "C. O. says differently. You made corporal." She took a pinch of qat and sealed the rest in her suit pocket, along with a little something extra for when they landed. She tucked the qat between her teeth and cheek before she pulled on her gloves.

"Field promotion because you refused to admit that last mission was your success, not mine."

Kay grabbed her helmet and turned her back to him. "Basic survival instinct." Leadership potential wasn't part of her gene-study, and she didn't go the extra kilometer for anyone but Jax. She had one goal every mission—stay alive, keep him alive. It was as simple as that.

The assembly deck held thirty drop ships, one per fire team for maximum maneuverability. Fifteen squads scrambled through the rows of ships to board. Kay's ship was the third in line, a tan oblong with atmospheric wings retracted and loading ramp extended. Jax nodded his approval to the deck crew and pilot as they finished their final prep for takeoff. They ignored him. Post-mission, she needed a serious talk with that Tarquin if he was going to keep up with this I'm-in-command crap.

Valderrama, their explosives expert, and the new kid were

already in their cramped section of the drop ship when she and Jax arrived. Valderrama was barrel-chested, middle-aged, and too proud for his own good. She knew nothing about the new kid except she was too young, too small, and too scared.

Kay slid into her seat next to Jax. She tightened the strap on her oxygen tank and spat out a stream of qat juice. It wouldn't be the worst thing the cleaning crew would scrub off the deck by the end of this mission. She turned to Jax. "How long?"

Jax slipped on his helmet. His eyes took on that distant look that meant he was accessing his Heads-Up Display. "HUD says fifteen minutes to drop."

Jax's mixed-breed Tarquin skin went even redder than normal as he fiddled with every strap and buckle on his suit and double-checked the line from his oxygen tank. His eyes flicked back and forth across his HUD, presumably as he scanned the status of every Marine under his command.

"You want some?" Kay tapped her traveling pharmacy sealed in her other suit pocket. She had a pill for every kind of mission and for the downtimes in between.

Jax shook his head. He was the only one who knew the extent of her stash. It was much better than the Neuro-X they gave every grunt to kill pain, and the Dexalin to stimulate coagulation on wounds.

Valderrama on the other hand, thought chewing qat was her main vice. "He's not desperate to look like a real Novan. You can chew qat and dye your hair black, but you're still pasty-faced Terran mierda."

Kay squeezed a stream spit through her teeth that landed on Valderrama's brown boots. "Whether I'm cloned from Terran shit or homegrown clanless Novan shit like you, it won't matter when the bullets fly, Private."

Valderrama's tanned face darkened in a rage that triggered an extra strong dose of his unique Novan scent. A dose like that from a woman would have had her weak in the knees. From him, it turned her stomach.

"Still sensitive about that demotion?" she said. "I can give you some pointers next time you go for a civilian."

"You're no better with women," he said through clenched teeth.

Kay's grin widened. "None of my dates ever filed charges against me."

That was one taunt too many for him. He lunged for her, but she was faster. She used his momentum to flatten him against the bulkhead and had her knife wrapped around his oxygen line before he could retaliate.

"You want to breathe on this mission," she said, "or does your pure Novan blood let you suck asteroid dust in place of air?"

Jax stepped in. "That's enough, Kay." When she didn't budge, he pulled rank. "Step down, Private First Class."

It was a direct order, but he'd managed a subtle dig by using her full rank, one grade above Valderrama's. Jax had her back, as always.

Kay let go of Valderrama's oxygen line, but she didn't sheathe her knife until he turned his back to her and maneuvered to the other end of their cramped space. She rolled her shoulders to let go of the tension and leaned back against her harness, spitting out the rest of her qat. The new kid's eyes were on her, but she was smart enough to keep out of it. Maybe she'd survive the first mission and earn the right to a name.

Kay wouldn't admit how much Valderrama's digs pissed her off. Her Terran origins isolated her even more than Jax's mixed-Tarquin blood. His was a fourth-generation gene line, closer to direct integration into the Novan gene pool. She was UT status—unaltered Terran, first-generation, from the Novan's worst enemy.

Terrans had tried to boot Novans out of the human race, and that wasn't something the Novans were inclined to forgive. Generations of Novan genetic manipulation made them physically and mentally superior, but no longer genetically pure as far as Terrans were concerned. Terrans compensated for being genetically left-behind with a heavy dependence on extensive integrated implants. They protected their genetic purity, while Novans made it all but sacrilegious to alter the human body with non-biological material.

Kay was in the middle of that mess, cloned from a Terran prisoner who caught the eye of the Nassien military establishment for exceptional natural combat skills. Jax had a similar background, but his gene line was further along. The Nassien Genetics Division mixed genes with other species like kids mixed paints in preschool, but Kay and Jax were the only two gene-line clones in the 28th Regiment. It was what made them closer than family to each other.

Kay locked on her helmet just as her comm came alive with a direct feed from their C.O. "Drop ship in five. Anyone who dies on this mission is on my shit list."

He wasn't a motivational speaker, but he'd kept most of them alive for the past seven months, all except Yang. Kay eyed up Yang's replacement. She didn't hold much hope for the kid. The new kid gave off a strong scent of fear, one that would have had Kay wrapping her in a protective bubble, if she hadn't long since learned how to control her instinctual Terran reaction to Novan scent variations. She hadn't let those scents control her since her first Novan girlfriend.

Novan pheromones were another one of those genetic differences between her and everyone else but Jax. No wonder they clung to each other like family. She couldn't detect and resist the effects of Novan pheromones on her without special modifications—modifications she got on the black market after being dumped by that girlfriend.

Jax settled down to a mild panic. "Countdown's starting. Strap in."

Kay buckled into her harness. The drop ship jolted seconds later as it was jettisoned from the belly of the *Kasai*. Her stomach dropped to her toes for an instant before their drop ship's engines kicked in and accelerated them toward their landing zone. She slipped a special green pill out of her pocket and tucked it under her upper lip. Prilax was a fast-acting stimulant. She wouldn't waste its effects until she had her automatic rifle pointed at something worth shooting.

"Shit!" Jax was on the private com to her, not a good sign.

"What's wrong?"

"Fourth fire team's drop ship malfunctioned. We're going in without them. How the hell are we supposed to keep going with a third less firepower?"

Kay's mind sped through their options and latched onto the best tactical alternative. "Order Valderrama to blow the hole. He and the kid stay behind to guard the exit while we join the Third fire team for the section-by-section sweep."

"She can't stay behind. She's your ammo backup."

Shit. Kay didn't want baby-sitting duties with the new kid, but a fire team had only so much flexibility. Jax was right; she needed the kid with her.

He squirmed out of his harness while he sent everyone their new mission responsibilities over their squad-com channel.

"What the hell are you doing?" she asked when he tore off his flak vest and tossed it at the new kid.

"It'll keep her alive," he said.

Kay wasn't going to take that bet. The kid looked like she was going to vomit in her helmet as she buckled up the oversized vest. This mission was going straight to hell, and they hadn't even landed yet.

The deck rumbled under Kay's boots. Landing gear down. The kid and Jax were back in their harness, and Valderrama was giving her the same look he did before every mission, the look that said, "Is this the one you're gonna turn on us, Terran bitch?"

She gave him back the same enigmatic smile she did on every mission. Let the bastard sweat a little.

She flicked on her HUD and watched their approach on the external camera feed. The asteroid's surface filled the view, a yellow-like beach sand, but this beach had too many boulders and no water. They approached the Jahan Depression, a relatively smooth plain where the ore was mined. The main mining pit, evident by the slag heap that rose thirty meters high above it, dominated the near side. The first mining dome rose from the surface like an off-white soap bubble. That was the target for a different squad, and she saw the distinct dots of those drop ships approaching it. Her target appeared on the horizon, smaller than the first dome, but marked by her HUD with three red dots. She didn't need them to see the defensive cannons visible above the dome. They were already active and targeting their ships. Neutralizing the cannons was her job, assuming they survived the landing.

"We're on the ground in ten," Jax said.

They were ten slow seconds as the drop ship dipped and swerved to avoid the cannon fire. If they were the original mining company cannons, and if they operated as badly as they had three months ago, and if the Terrans hadn't upgraded them, Kay and her squad would survive. It was a lot of ifs.

One final steep dive ended in a teeth-jarring thud. They were dirt-bound. Kay was first out of her harness and at the exit hatch, waiting for the go signal from Jax. She switched her multi-ammo rifle to nuclear bullets and started sucking air through her helmet's oxygen feed. Jax gave her the nod, and she slapped the hatch trigger at the same time she bit into the Prilax pill.

The world slowed as Kay's mind sped from the first rush of the drug. She could feel every heartbeat, every blink of her eyes like she was watching it all on slow motion video. She had the first cannon in her sites before the hatch finished sliding open. With the cockiness of unmatched firing accuracy, she fired a single round and shifted to line up the second cannon before her HUD registered the hit and explosion of the first. She neutralized the second just as easily. The third got off one round before Kay blasted the cannon to bits. Not even her drug-enhanced reflexes could shoot down the incoming ordinance.

She and Valderrama were out of the hatch before the explosion took out the front of their drop ship. So much for the pilot. She looked back to see the new kid on the deck with Jax sprawled across her. Always the freaking hero.

"If you're not in heat, get off the kid and get out here," she said on their private channel. He grunted in reply and rolled off. After a spot check of his gear and the kid's, they were out beside Kay. Jax looked back at the mess of their ship. Even the hero knew there was no hope for their pilot. He'd blame himself for that one.

He turned back to them. "Station-safe ammo."

As the only one firing outside the dome, Kay was the only squad member needing to switch ammo packs. She pulled out her nuke pack and switched it with the station-safe pack the kid held out for her.

Valderrama and Jax popped up an emergency dome extension, large enough for one person. With the extension in place, the dome would not register a loss of atmospheric pressure when they blew the hatch. Valderrama was already tacking the explosives to the maintenance hatch when Third fire team landed behind their ruined ship. Kay's HUD registered the presence of four more friendlies as Third fire team exited their ship. They were all under Jax's command and awaited orders.

On Jax's signal, Valderrama blew a hole in the hatch. He crawled out of the emergency dome extension in a cloud of dust. "Atmosphere secure." He was a jackass, but he was good at what he did.

"Everyone in." Jax started to lead the way, but Kay shoved him back.

She slapped his unprotected bio suit. "You're on hatch watch, remember?" She couldn't see his face but she knew he was regretting his decision to stay behind with Valderrama. Too late for second thoughts.

Kay crawled through the hole first and grabbed the ladder that led down into the underground facility. "Come on, kid."

Kay's HUD switched to overlay a map of the maintenance tunnels they were heading into. She registered the new kid at her back and four more following her down the ladder.

CHAPTER 2

Gene Study – KDTU-02128 Project Initiation-3046 AH

Nassien Military Research Division received preliminary concept approval for gene line designate KDTU-02128. Gene expression profiling was initiated on a batch of 700 blastocysts with an 83% success ratio. Second stage proceeded on 150 embryos for selective gene blocking. This stage was inconclusive with 63% showing extreme sensitivity to the procedure ending in early terminations. The project received funding for a repeat second stage and used an experimental gene blocking procedure on the next batch of embryos. Four preliminary target gene sets were identified. The project is scheduled to move into third stage cloning in 3047 AH with approval for an initial batch of ten replicants (Gen 3, Crèche D).

Prilax settled in Kay's system with a steady mid-range stim level that would last at least two hours, enough time to live or die on this mission. She dropped from the ladder and scanned the tunnel in both directions. Nothing. The tunnel had the bare minimum for access lighting, but it was enough. Her HUD map directed her to the right, and she trotted down that direction with the kid at her heels. The two of them took up position at the first intersection. Her HUD registered nothing but the background hum of the overhead pipes.

Two from the Third fire team leapfrogged in front. So far so good, but this was the easy part. The Terrans wouldn't have had enough prior warning to set up live resistance in the maintenance tunnels. The only risk was if they'd mined it. Forward progress was limited to two guinea pigs at a time.

A dull series of leapfrogs later, and they made it to the facility entrance.

"In position," Kay said over the comm link to Jax.

"No situational updates from here," he said. "Stay alive."

Kay looked back at the combined team. "Final ammo check."

She checked the kid's ammo herself. No way was she sucking asteroid dust because the new kid didn't know the difference between station-safe and hull-blasting bullets. The rest of the team gave her the thumbs up. Everyone was ready.

She was blind to what was on the other side of the hatch. It should be the chamber for the unmanned cyclone mineral separators, but given the number of bunker-buster bombs the Terrans had fired on this asteroid to "soften up the resistance," there could be anything from a gaping hole into space, to an operational separator chugging away at asteroid rock to produce a steady stream of usable ore and disposable slag.

One way to find out. She waved Third fire team's strongest grunt forward. "Let's go."

He started pulling on the manual hatch lever. The hatch had to be at least five centimeters thick as it rose vertically over Kay's head. A stream of smoke seeped into their tunnel from the opening. Not a good sign.

When the hatch was less than halfway up, Kay crawled into the chamber with the kid once again on her heels. There were only two sounds Kay could make out—the loud groan of mechanical equipment still running and the unmistakable ping of enemy fire. She scrambled for cover. The kid didn't.

The first two in from the Third fire team shoved the kid in Kay's direction. They found their own safety behind the biggest metal pipe Kay had ever seen—at least twice the width of the hatch. The kid managed to drag herself behind Kay, while the rest of Third fire team spread out on either side of the hatch.

Kay's HUD registered breathable air, and she switched off her oxygen line. Waste not, want not, and who knew what portions of the mining camp would lose oxygen before the mission was completed.

The place smelled of grease and dirt. She didn't know if the cloud of smoke around them was a side effect of the cyclone separator at work or because the facility had taken one too many hits from space. Either way, it definitely wasn't unmanned now.

"We're in," she said. "Multiple enemies registering on HUD."

"I see seven," Jax said. As squad leader, he could network all their HUD output into his own. "I need a wider angle to pinpoint locations."

Kay gave the signal, and the team spread further out, scrambling around the outer perimeter of the chamber. She dragged the kid with her, using one of the massive inlet pipes for protection. Everything was covered in a greasy layer of muck, even the floor. Her brown bio suit was soot-black on the arms and legs, but nothing as bad as the kid, who'd spent more time sprawled on the ground than any sane Marine should.

"I got 'em," Jax said. "Sending back target data now."

Kay's HUD dimmed out the other enemies and tracked on two, one fifteen meters in front of her and another thirty degrees to her right. The kid's HUD would show the same. "I'm on the right, you take forward."

She moved out, trusting her HUD output to keep her alive. It tracked both target enemies. It also tracked the kid, who was sticking to her like glue instead of taking out the alternate target. Stupid frigging kid.

She fired a few random rounds to shake up her first target. The Terran scrambled in the wrong direction, and Kay fired off one perfect shot.

Her HUD showed only one enemy now, at her left and dangerously close. The kid should have neutralized that one, if she hadn't been too young and too stupid. Kay popped a shock grenade off to her left and dove to her right, dragging the useless kid with her. The energy wave flattened them and blanked out her HUD. It would come back in a minute or two, but that was long enough to end up dead.

"Running blind," she said through her com link. The kid was still with her, curled up behind a conveyor belt wheel and looking like she was going to vomit.

"Cross-correlating Third fire team HUDs," Jax said. She heard the strain in his voice. He wasn't the type to remotely control a battle. He needed to be on the inside. So did she. "Okay, you're clear for now. Maintain position until your HUD reboots."

She looked down at the kid, who had a bad case of the hiccups now. The kid hadn't fired a shot, a bad sign if she wanted to survive her first mission. Battle shock wasn't going to keep either of them alive.

Kay's HUD came back on, and she registered one last enemy, still flat out from the shock grenade. She grabbed the front of the kid's bio suit. "You see that enemy dot on your HUD?"

The kid nodded.

"Kill it." She let the kid go and waited. Five seconds. Ten seconds. On her Prilax rush, it felt like an eternity while the kid just cried. Sympathy wasn't strong in Kay's gene line. She pulled her pistol out and aimed it at the kid. "Kill it or I kill you. I'm not real picky which right now."

Amazing how fast a bullet can motivate even the young and stupid. The kid shouldered her rifle, but didn't take aim the way a sane person would. Instead, she flipped to auto-fire and ran screaming around the equipment, spraying bullets everywhere.

Jax was screaming in her ear a second later. "Kay! What's happening?"

Kay sprang up and followed the trail of bullets. "They gave us a green kid, that's what's happening." She passed the bullet-ridden corpse of the last enemy in their immediate vicinity but the kid was already out the far hatch and tracking down an unsecured passageway.

"Fourth fire team just landed," Jax said. "Hold position until we get there."

"I would if we had a position to hold." She spun around the final conveyor and bolted out the hatch less than two seconds after the kid. The stream of bullets ended. Kay checked her HUD. It tracked no live enemies directly ahead, and only one friendly. The lucky little shit survived.

Kay stepped over two bodies before she found the kid sitting on the floor next to another body, her rifle at her feet. The tears were gone. In their place were full-body tremors. The shock of first kill, or in this case, first four kills. From slacker to overachiever. The kid would either speed her way through the ranks, or snap and kill everyone. It was the same future every clanless Novan brat faced in their first year in the war.

Kay picked up the kid's rifle and handed it back to her. "This keeps you alive. Never let it go."

The kid took it, but her eyes never left the corpse next to her.

Kay interposed herself between the two, breaking that eye contact, and turned on her comm link. "Position secure, passageway five."

They were joined by the Third fire team, and within five minutes, Jax and Valderrama. No one mentioned the kid's near-catatonic state.

"Control room ahead. We go by twos," Jax said. "Kay, you're with Valderrama."

The leapfrog took them down two more well lit but vacant passageways. The kid trailed along well enough, but Kay wouldn't trust she had her back. They paused in front of the final hatch as Valderrama set the charge. It was a well-shielded room, so they were once again going in blind.

When the charge blew, Kay jumped forward. Valderrama was at her heels, cursing her but not ready to assume she'd turned traitor just yet.

At least it kept Jax and the kid out of the line of fire, she thought. She eliminated the first two targets, but the room had more enemy beacons than a Terran military parade. She and Valderrama lay down a steady protective fire. The next two through the hatch were Jax and the kid. They should have stopped two meters in front of Kay, but the kid didn't stop at all and neither did he. Frigging Jax.

Kay's HUD registered at least twenty enemy targets. She picked them off as fast as Prilax and instinct could carry her, but it wasn't enough. She was never enough. Her HUD registered the elimination of her seventh target simultaneous with the warning beacon that their squad leader was hit. Jax was down.

As second in command, her HUD lit up instantly with the networked input from the rest of her squad. The Novan military followed strict protocol when a leader was down. Next in line got full resources to carry the mission through. Kay didn't give a damn about that protocol.

"Valderrama, pull Third forward and secure the room!" She scrambled forward between bodies and equipment until she found Jax. The kid was squatting over his still form, firing away, but this time, one precise bullet at a time. Kay's HUD showed three less enemy targets.

"He's alive." The kid eliminated her fourth target.

Kay pulled up Jax's vitals on her HUD. He was alive. His normal heart rate was half her own, but now it registered a third less than normal. He needed a medic, but the son-of-a-bitch Tarquin was too big for her to carry, even with the kid's help.

"Valderrama!"

"Busy here, Terran," Valderrama said over their comm link.

"We're pulling back. I need you to haul Jax out of here."

"We hold the control room. That's our mission."

Tarquin blood stained the floor around Jax. "Command goes to me, not you, Private. Abort!"

Valderrama cursed, but he was at her side in less than half a minute. He'd screw her over in the post-mission debrief, but Jax would be safe, no matter what. If the damned Tarquin mongrel would stop bleeding so much.

Valderrama gave Jax a fast once-over, his face registering the vast quantities of blood.

Kay turned back to the kid, who was still systematically eliminating any enemies that exposed themselves. "You're with me. We sweep the tunnels back to the surface. Valderrama takes Jax. Third fire team, fall back by twos."

Third fire team gave them cover as Valderrama hoisted Jax over his shoulder. Kay reconnected her oxygen line and verified Jax's line was still attached. Frigging hero never had a chance to switch off. She didn't bother checking the kid's. Let someone else baby sit. The kid had caused enough damage already.

"Move." Kay led the way back to their damaged ship. She switched her comm to the med channel and gave them the heads-up she was bringing Jax in. They'd already be reading his vitals. She just hoped the medevac ship wasn't too far off. It was a hell of a lot of blood.

The return trip through the maze of passageways seemed to take forever. Prilax remained as active as ever, whether she was in the middle of battle, or running like a scared rabbit down the nearest hole. Mission clock gave them less than twenty minutes in. She was going to be a twitchy wreck until she got the chance to counter the drug with something else.

They passed beyond the confines of the dome just as the Medevac ejected a hover-gurney for Jax. The self-propelled gurney landed ten meters away. Valderrama deposited Jax down on the gurney. The flow of blood was already slowing down. Automatic sensors restrained him and started vital sign verification and initial triage. Less than a minute later, the gurney lifted off and began its return journey to the Medevac ship.

Kay's HUD displayed a running update of his status from the gurney. Heart rate had stabilized, and blood pressure returned to Tarquin normal. The quick-healing bastard would be okay. She likely just bought herself a demotion to match Valderrama's for aborting the mission so close to success. If she cared, she could bring up her HUD archives to see how close they were to success. If she cared.

The ground rumbled beneath her feet.

Valderrama grunted. "So much for the mission."

That put the final seal on her screw-up. The Terrans had blown the control room. All that machinery would be grinding to a halt. This asteroid's mine wouldn't be making a profit any time soon.

Third and Fourth fire team hailed their drop ships and evacuated the asteroid. Kay, Valderrama, and the kid had to cool their heels and wait for a cleanup ship to come fetch them. She let her drop ship get crippled, her best friend get shot, and her mission fail. Even for her, this was a record-breaking day.

She wanted qat or something stronger from her personal pharmacy, but she'd suck it up until she got on the rescue ship. The sole benefit of being a gene line experiment meant they could only demote her so far. Even a misfit like her couldn't be booted entirely out of the Nassien Military establishment. They'd already spent too much money raising her, stuffing her in military training at the age of eight, and running endless experiments on her mental capacity, reflexes, and who knows what else. No, she wasn't going anywhere but down a pay grade.

The kid looked like she was barely holding on to sanity. Her fists were tight around her gun and her eyes never left the opening they'd blown into the dome, even though the access tunnels had probably cratered in from the control room explosion. First missions.

How do you prep a kid for blasting a hole in someone's chest? Kay still had squad-control and switched her helmet comm to a private link with the kid. "He'll live."

The kid flinched, but had enough sense to keep her response private as well. "How do you know?"

"He's a gene line Experimental. His gene line's goal is to

improve on the Tarquin fast-healing abilities. He won't die from a couple of station-safe shots." It was the mantra she kept repeating to herself. He was as close to family as she was ever going to get. The bastard better stay alive.

The kid didn't look much better. Her almond-shaped eyes dominated her pixie face. A trace of her straight black hair had slipped down across her cheek. Long hair and helmets weren't a good combination.

"How old are you?" Kay asked.

"Sixteen."

A year older than Kay was for her first mission, but Novans matured slower than Terrans. The kid really was just a kid. "How'd you end up in this mess?"

"My family sold me to the Nassiens a year ago."

The kid's voice had no hint of anger or regret. It was a common story for the clanless, and for some of them, a better future than the ones they left behind. If they lived long enough to see that future.

"How'd you get here?" the kid asked.

"Same as Jax, lucky Terran gene line." Kay wasn't an Experimental though; she was an Unaltered, with no fancy upgrades to her flat-out boring Terran genetics, a direct clone.

"You don't look Terran."

It was almost a compliment on how well Kay masked her blonde roots and blue eyes, but it was more likely that the kid was just off some backwater farming planet and had never seen Terrans beyond the propaganda vids.

Valderrama broke in on an open squad channel. "Are you done warping the kid's mind? Because our ship's on its way in."

Kay stood up and switched to an open squad channel. "What's your name, kid?"

"Ysabet. Sorry, I forgot your name."

"She hasn't got a name, just a designation," Valderrama said. "What is it again? K-D-T-U and a bunch of numbers, right Terran?"

She was too wired to bother with the insult dance, and he was right, she and Jax didn't have names, just gene line designations. Why humanize an experimental project?

"Kay works." She held out her hand. "Here comes our lift, Ysabet."

Wasn't much of a pep talk, but Kay wasn't much of a talker. The kid got her name back. It was the standard military grunt recognition that you'd survived your first mission and earned your way onto the fire team.

CHAPTER 3

Gene Study – KDTU-02128 Replicant Status-3049 AH

Nassien Military Research Division third stage cloning of gene line KDTU-02128 proceeding with 70% success rating in first two years. Surviving replicants of Crèche D began gene set enrichment analysis, the results of which will be used in later-stage stimulation of the profile genes. Test case application and gene set verification expected by 3050 AH. Fourth-stage cloning approval gated by the successful identification of gene sets critical to the gene line trait isolation.

"No demotion?" Jax asked, again. His red hue was back to experimental Tarquin normal, making him look out of place wrapped in stiff white sheets in a hospital bunk and surrounded by beeping machinery.

Kay spat qat juice into an empty cup she nabbed off his meal tray. "Disappointed?"

He swallowed the remnants of his nutrient-rich, flavor-poor breakfast bun. "No, just surprised. Valderrama's not too happy about it. He thought he had you with this one."

Kay rested her boots on his hospital bunk where he was recovering faster than any sane person would want to. At this rate, he'd be back on active duty in a week. "Someone besides me must have thought it was worth abandoning the mission to save your red hide."

For all the fun she got out of her free ride, she knew deep down it wasn't free. Someone pulled strings to keep her out of trouble, and that was a debt that would come back to haunt her someday. Nobody in the Nassien establishment did favors out of the kindness of their hearts.

Five other bunks made up the rest of this hospital ward, one of ten on board. Three of the other bunks were already vacated, grunts with less-critical injuries than Jax had. Kay glanced at the two occupied bunks. One of them was in a forced coma. The other probably wished she was, given what was left of her extremities wasn't a pretty sight, even from a distance. Kay hated hospital wards.

"When you getting out of that bunk, anyway?" she asked.

"Another three days, and I'm back on picket duty with the rest of you."

"Sucks to be a quick healer."

Jax shrugged. "I wouldn't be here if I wasn't."

Kay spat the rest of her qat into the cup. It didn't pay to dwell on why they were here or anywhere. They weren't the product of passionate romance, or even a quickie in a closet. Lab rats didn't get that much. Their miracle of birth had been through cell cloning and growth in a species-variant artificial replicator.

She swung her legs back to the deck and left the cup on his meal tray for the orderly to deal with. "Don't rush on my account. These balls of dirt are even less interesting than your luxury accommodations are here."

He grimaced as she got up and left the ward. Even Mr. Optimistic didn't like the picket duty.

They spent the next three long weeks on the mining colony asteroid before the permanent infantry company arrived to take over. Then it was another month on a cramped Marine transport back to the New China system with nothing to do but eat, shit, and sleep.

They were going home. Not just Marine home, but real home. New China was not only a major Novan solar system, it was the central system controlled and managed by the Nassien Autonomy. She and Jax were but small offshoots from the military-scientific branch of that vast family-controlled leviathan. It existed somewhere between corporate entity, regional tribe, and military juggernaut. Big, powerful, and it owned her ass. Still she was grown and spat out from a replicator in the New China system, so for all intents and purposes, it was home to her.

Ysabet didn't get over her first battle nightmares, as Kay knew only too well because they all bunked in the same closet. She didn't know what was worse, Valderrama's Novan scent that smelled like old boots or Ysabet's crying in her sleep. Jax tried the big-brother shoulder to cry on approach but that didn't help.

Two days before their scheduled landing, Kay took Ysabet aside outside their assigned arms locker and tried a different approach.

"When we dock, you go to this suite." Kay pulled her datapad out of her hip pocket and synced it to Ysabet's to transfer over the relevant info.

Ysabet looked at her datapad. "What is this place?"

"A sex parlor. I know the owner, she'll take good care of you, whatever your preferences are." In fact, Kay would likely hook up with the owner herself when they arrived in-system.

Ysabet ducked her chin to make her straight black hair block her reddening cheeks. "I don't think I'm allowed in a place like that."

Kay tapped the rifle that Ysabet was cleaning. "That's your ticket in. The minute you took that up, you became a legal Novan adult." She put her arm over Ysabet's shoulder. "Sex, drugs, drinks. It's all fair game now."

Ysabet's normally cinnamon-like Novan scent became something else. Kay had seduced enough Novan women to recognize that change, but she didn't step back right away. At least the kid was thinking beyond her first kill for once, even if nothing would ever happen between them. Shit, the kid was three physical years younger than Kay, and five or more mental years younger. Never gonna happen.

"Just try it out. Good people there." Kay locked up her own firearms and left Ysabet to think about it. *You can lead a girl to some great action, but you can't force her to enjoy it.*

Their transport docked at Massalia, the Marine transfer station in the Ring, a series of artificial planetoids in solar orbit beyond the seven major habitable planets of the New China system. The view port to Kay's left showed two of those planets, full sized, and a third as a slim red crescent. She'd never been allowed access beyond the Ring, but it was the best view she would get until she got planet-side.

Kay hoisted her duffel bag over her shoulder and joined Jax and the stream of Marines filing out of the transport, all dressed in well-worn brown fatigues. She spotted a few blue-clad ship personnel attempting to control the mass exodus. Why did they ever bother? Marines on leave would figure out the fastest way off ship without the Navy getting in the way.

The Massalia station was designed for function, not aesthetic beauty, as a series of concentric levels around a central cylinder of machinery that kept the station functional. Docking bays protruded from that core like legs on a centipede, with ships like theirs locked at the tip of most of them. Still, the sterile scent of the docking bay, even with the smell escaping from the dockside sanitation processing, was heaven compared to the month-old stench of Marines post-deployment.

"What are you doing first," Jax asked, "Shower, food, or sex?"

Kay sniffed herself. "Last one's not an option till the first one's done. How about you?"

"Food."

"That's got to suck, only being in heat when the right female tags you with her scent."

Jax shrugged. "Saves me the kind of problems you and Valderrama get yourselves into."

He had a point, especially after Ysabet's recent reactions. Coming back to home base presented its own complications to her sex life. She'd been through most of the locals already, and those who didn't hate her, stalked her for attention the moment she landed.

Her datapad buzzed in her pocket right on cue as soon as they cleared the EM blocking field on the transport. Jax's buzzed at the same time.

"You stealing my girls?" She scanned her pad and read her messages. The first three were from the expected stalker-dates, but the last one was even worse. It was from Halabi, her gene line program manager. "Looks like our PM is working overtime. Mandatory blood test and a pre-scheduled visit at 14:00 hours. You got something better going on?"

Jax frowned at his datapad. "Same here, but I have until tomorrow. It's not like Halabi to go through the expense of a face to face meeting."

"Yeah." That wasn't the only anomaly. Her meeting was on Kendari, one of the outer planetoids in the Ring, and as far away as possible from the lab that kept tabs on her, and subsequently housed Halabi's cramped office. She visited Kendari regularly, but it wasn't the sort of place she wanted her PM to know about, or Jax for that matter. What she did there wasn't strictly legal, especially for a gene line clone. The Nassien Genetic Research Division wouldn't take kindly to any tampering with their gene lines, but Kendari was the best place in the New China system for black market gene doping. Had Halabi caught on to it? She was promised nothing would ever show up in her periodic gene tests, but there were always risks.

Jax shoved his datapad back in his pocket. "You think he's going to separate us? The Research Division doesn't like stationing gene lines in the same squad." The unvoiced question—was this the price they would pay because Kay screwed a mission to save his hide?

She shook her head. "If he wanted to skin us for the mission, why step in and save my rank?" She'd worked out over the dull trip back that only a pre-stated requirement from her PM could have prevented her automatic demotion. Her C.O. wouldn't have spared her, that was for sure.

She and Jax on the same squad were an anomaly, one that

Halabi reminded her of regularly, as if it meant she owed him one. If he knew she was experimenting with gene doping, would he punish her by separating her from Jax? That wasn't a bridge Kay wanted to cross any time soon.

"I don't think he'll pull one of us. Fire teams take time to gel, and we just got Ysabet. He'd have split us before, when we lost Yang." For all Valderrama was a dick, he was a dick she'd already broken in. Another fire team would mean breaking a few bones to establish herself, and she'd never had to do that without Jax at her back. They'd been paired from the start, but for what reasons, she didn't know.

Thinking about it was a waste anyway. They both had Property of Nassien Military stamped on their asses. They'd go wherever their owners sent them.

"Still, haven't seen Halabi face to face in over two years. Something's up." Jax gave her a sideways glance. "Are you clean?"

"Always." At least she'd kept clean of the more restricted drugs during her month-long ship time. Her tests would be relatively clean. Halabi shouldn't have anything concrete on her. Not that it would stop him from jerking either of them around. He'd always had a vindictive edge he took out on them if he was in the mood. Or bored. Or recently chewed out by his boss, wife, parents, bank clerk, anybody. The guy had the personality of asteroid dust.

She looked at the time. Three hours. Enough time for shower and food, or shower and sex.

She'd had a big enough breakfast to hold her for a while.

HALABI STARED AT Kay across a sticky bar table in one of the more run-down bars on Kendari. She knew just how run down, since she came to Kendari every six months for reasons she hoped Halabi didn't know. This particular bar skimped on both the lighting and the building air purifiers. Kendari wasn't a rich planetoid since its legal economy centered on cheap labor and lax worker safety regulations. That meant it had minimal government revenue to spend on things like air quality and environmental upkeep. Less-seedy bars paid for air purifiers to make up for the government shortfalls, but not this place.

She'd never met up with her PM outside a military base, and she didn't think Halabi selected this establishment for its atmosphere. Then again, looking at the multiple dark corners and overall lack of military presence, maybe he had. None of this was good. Kay knew the military, knew where the lines were drawn and which ones she could cross and get away with. She was out of her depth, and the smirk on Halabi's face as he sipped his Turkish coffee said he knew it, too.

Halabi's voice was scratchy from the bad air as he ground out the vitals of Kay's gene line. "You're stalling." You meaning all of Kay's line. No PM ever told her how many more there were, and Halabi, being the latest of a line of PMs hoping to use the gene line program as a stepping stone to promotion, wasn't about to fill her in either. She could have one gene-sister or a thousand. Not that it mattered. She'd never see any of them.

"Kay." Halabi leaned back in the synthwood booth and folded his hands. His face contorted into what might have been a smile. How could a man who couldn't be over thirty Novan-standard, not have the facial muscles to pull off a believable smile? There was some serious bitterness in this man. "Do you know how many of your line call themselves Kay?"

It wasn't a real question, and he wasn't going to give her a real answer. Just another one of his weak attempts to draw her in, get her to take the bait. She'd had enough screwball project managers over the years. His attempts were weaker than most. She just drank her beer from what felt like a real glass mug and waited for him to make his point.

Halabi pulled out his datapad and tapped on a display Kay couldn't see. "According to the initial gene study, you should be three grade levels above what you are now." He peered at

Kay. "Four if I hadn't overridden your demotion for the Xi fiasco."

So it was true. He'd made sure she'd keep her grade. There was some forethought to that, given the delay in trans-system communications. Nobody had called him from Xi, so that meant he'd put some rider in her record preventing any demotion. People didn't step out on a limb for her, except Jax, unless they wanted something. There wasn't anything she had that Halabi could want, unless he was going to just push her up through the ranks to prove he was making a success out of her line. Was it a fast track to some higher rank she had no interest in?

Then again, it could just be another of his psych tests. Either way, higher rank wasn't in her short list of goals. She toyed with the moisture ring her sweating beer mug left on the scarred table between them. "Maybe I'm not fit for military duty."

"Oh, you're fit. You're all fit." He stared at his datapad again like it held some mysterious answer that would click her and the rest of her line in gear. "Less than fifteen percent survival rate past thirty. Tell me, is that a suicide streak in your gene line we haven't detected?"

Fifteen percent. No wonder she focused on the now. She didn't have a future. Twelve years to go. She chugged her beer, better make the best of it.

He sighed. "Your gene line is fucked, you know that? Some Nassien bureaucrat bought into the notion that a Terran P.O.W. had superpowers for situational awareness, and they've been trying to bleed that out of your gene line for decades. I'm sick of dead KDTUs. The paperwork's a bitch."

Kay couldn't mask the shock. He wasn't supposed to be telling her any of this. Eighteen years, and no one had ever let slip why her gene line existed. As a kid, she'd asked every new PM. Only one ever acknowledged the question and even that one had waved it off with vague comments about it being a blind study, and to know would skew results. So why was it okay that she knew now? And what was in it for Halabi, who'd been her PM for enough years now that whatever fast track he was hoping for in his career wasn't happening through her.

He took another sip of his coffee. "You like this place? Don't bother answering. I know about your trips to Kendari. Everything you do is recorded. I also have a good idea of what you do here, though you're smart enough not to leave any detectable record. That's why I picked this place." He waved his hand. "No recordings."

She looked around the bar again. He was right, the omnipresent two-way vid links and mobile street cams were nowhere in sight. Just the two of them, a robot barkeep, and an intoxicated local slumped in the far corner booth. Way too isolated for her taste. She didn't like it. *Situational awareness my ass.* She felt trapped in some unknown web Halabi was spinning. It wasn't a good feeling at all. "What's your point?"

He leaned forward, his grey business suit straining at the seams. Someone had gained weight recently. "My point is I don't care what you do to your body or your gene line. Like I said, it's all been a colossal waste. A pipe-dream that's stagnating my career and killing off your relatives, if you can call them that. Can you even understand the idea of family, of blood bond? Maybe not."

He was pushing the family button a lot in this conversation, but was it hers or his that was preying on his mind? The psych test could go both ways. She tossed out her own bait. "How much help has your family been to you?"

His expression turned glacial. *Gotcha*, she thought. As usual, this had nothing to do with her, and everything to do with him.

"Your next deployment could be a real interesting one, for you and me both. You'll get mission details from your C.O, but I'll tell you this one thing, you'll get to meet your owner."

Owner. It was a figurative term, since she was owned by the Nassien Military Corporation, but she got the hint. One of the high-ranking Nassien clan was going to lead her next mission. "Why should I care?"

He slapped his cup down on its saucer hard enough to crack it. "I'd terminate your whole gene line if I could. Every last one of you gets under my skin."

She waited him out. He had a point to make, and she wasn't going to feed it to him. She didn't trust the bastard not to be recording their chat anyway, though why he would was beyond her. This whole clandestine conversation was beyond her, and it wasn't a situation she was used to. The sooner he called this chat over, the better.

He settled the cup more stably on its saucer. The crack in it showed that, like her glass mug, the saucer was from natural materials. Quite the retro bar he'd found, but maybe that was what ensured there were no surreptitious recording devices. "Okay, here's why you should care. You're going to die in this military outfit. Maybe not this mission, maybe not the next, but I gave you the stats. Your gene line has no superpowers. It was a royal cockup from the start, and nobody has the 'nads to accept that. There's nothing you can do about it, nothing I can do about it. But this mission? This is probably your only chance to eek a little revenge."

Revenge he wanted to enjoy through her. She wondered what this Nassien offshoot had done to piss him off this much. Jilted lover? Family rival? Hell, given his reaction to her family bait, maybe he was related to the Nassiens. Wouldn't be that far-fetched an idea, given how long the Nassien Autonomy had been around and how many sub tribes had hitched a ride on that superpower wagon over the centuries.

He sipped the last dregs of his coffee, as if letting his words settle on in. "You and I, we don't pretend to like each other, and that's fine, but we have one thing in common—no reason to like the woman who's going to be your mission commander."

So it was a woman and a Nassien. Jilted lover. She gave Halabi a quick study again—shoulder-length black hair that curled over the top of his dress suit, narrow, dark eyes, and aquiline nose. Not particularly ugly, if you liked men.

He stood up to leave. "Let's just say if you manage to screw up this mission like you did the last, maybe we'd both get a little something out of it. Hell, you do a good enough job, and maybe we can convince the bureaucrats that you're all just a waste of money." He synced his datapad to the shop and paid the bill. "Freedom for your gene line. What's it worth to you?"

She traced her finger in the condensation on her beer bottle as she watched him leave. She had another hour before she could catch a shuttle back to base, plenty of time to chew over what he had and hadn't told her. She waited until he slipped into his rented air car and zipped up out of view. Then she got up and ordered something stronger than beer and took a booth closer to the street view. The area was a block-by-block grid of derelict buildings, with the occasional ramshackle establishment like this one popping up to serve the lowest dredges of Kendari society. Not many locals were around though, given it was the middle of day shift.

Halabi obviously hated whoever this new Nassien was, enough to go out on this limb and indirectly suggest mission sabotage. He had to be related to the Nassiens or he wouldn't be in charge of some of their gene lines, so that suggested he had a personal grudge against this particular Nassien. Family meant everything to Novans, so going against family meant some powerful motivator. He was definitely the type to not take rejection well. Maybe he tried to marry his way to a better career and she turned him down? That might be enough to like her already.

The other thing he said without saying was this had to be one hell of a mission if it brought in military brass from the ruling family.

She polished off her shot of whiskey and wished she'd gotten Halabi to pay for a meal when he was in his generous mood. Her stomach protested the meal she'd given up in place of a visit to that sex parlor. She'd wait to eat back on the base.

She had better things to spend her money on, like her trip back down here to Kendari before their redeployment.

THE MILITARY GENETICS lab on Massalia station was located on the third ring out from the core, fifth level, its white-and-gray front nestled between a tacky Ring souvenir shop and the station's best synthburger joint. It was a relatively small facility, the main labs being located planet-side. It was convenient though, allowing the researchers to poke and prod their lab rats between missions without the added cost to shuttle them off station. Kay showed up at the lab with Jax at her side. She hadn't offered any information on her meeting with Halabi and, for once, Jax seemed too distracted to ask.

The smell from the burger joint triggered a rumbling in Kay's stomach. She nodded in its direction. "You want to grab a bite first?"

"Yeah, sure." Jax glanced where she pointed. "Oh, now? Can't. I'm up for my annual test cycle."

Distracted for sure. He could eat her and half a squad under the table. And that was when he wasn't hungry.

He paused at the side hatch to the lab, the one marked with a red-and-black biohazard label that they made the classified gene lines use. "You ever wonder what our lives would be like if we weren't in this program?"

Kay shook her head and pushed past him through the lab hatch. "You ever wonder what it would be like to piss through your nose?" It was her way of saying it was a stupid question. They were who they were and nothing was going to change that.

The beige passageway had convenient color-coded wall stripes to direct each gene line type to the correct processing lab—red for Tarquin, brown for Terran, green for Aquarans, orange, yellow, and purple. She'd never seen anyone following the black line, but then there were no Black March freaks in the Marines. They were special forces and never mixed with the grunts, but she saw Jax looking down the passageway where the black line led. "Stop obsessing over them."

"Easy for you to say when your gene line is still Unaltered. I'm already an Experimental. They spin a new gene line generation every three years." He looked down the passageway, again. "Who's to say some of me isn't already down there."

"Who's to say your gene line isn't a raging success and they've already stolen what they wanted from your gene-set and boxed the rest?" She slapped him on the back. "You could just be the last dredges they're too lazy to dump in the bin."

"You always know the right thing to say." He gave her a half-hearted smile and followed his red line down the opposite passageway. "See you in a few hours."

He obsessed over his gene line too much. What did it matter if there were other versions of him floating around, with different genetic tweaks? They'd have to survive on their own, just like he did.

Or not survive, like her gene line seemed to be doing. She thought back to when she was ten years old. She'd spent most of her early years in military school getting the snot kicked out of her, but by the time she was ten, she'd learned how to fight back. She'd also learned how to fudge the tests so she didn't come out on top. Nothing she did would have justified running another generation of her gene line, that was for sure. She was probably the dredge of her own gene-set.

Kay followed the brown stripe down a long passageway and up a stairwell. She passed lab techs, who ignored her, and other Terran lab rats, who studied her in the same quick glance she gave them. Lab experiments had a way of eyeing each other up in an instant and storing the details away. She'd never spoken to one, nor they to her. It was an unwritten code among them. As the most hated of foreign species, it did them no good to seem eager to meet up. The only thing she'd learned from all her glancing studies was that lab rats never made it to old age. Maybe they all had an unconscious suicide streak.

Kay turned a corner in the passageway, ignoring all the

closed hatches along the way. They were either empty, or in use by other Terran gene lines. She reported into the first open hatch on the left and punched in her designation. The gene line rooms were larger than a normal exam room. This room sported the usual exam table, side chair that no one sat on, and simple monitoring tools. The room also accommodated five different test stations where they would measure everything and anything. Kay hopped up on the table and waited.

Twenty minutes later, a short, dark-haired lab technician with an extra-wide midsection came in the room. "KDTU-02128-4-H." She had an unpleasant squeak for a voice.

Kay nodded and stripped off her brown fatigues. The lab tech took blood and saliva samples and then plugged Kay into the first of five test stations. They'd test everything from brain waves to vision to heart-lung reactions and blood oxygen levels. Everything to prove she remained untampered, which of course, she wasn't.

Her first effort to tamper with nature came in the form of a pheromone blocker after getting shafted by her first girlfriend. It worked like a dream, until test station 3 picked up the modification, and she'd gotten more than an earful about genetic tampering being off-limits for her, a harsh rule in a society obsessed with gene-based human enhancements.

Lucky for her, the black market usually kept one step ahead of the government-sanctioned genetics labs, if one knew where to do business, and she did. She did her homework after that first screw-up and started with a base set of blood oxygen enhancers, and then selected a few cognitive improvements. Luckily, she'd kept that set at a minimum. If Halabi was telling the truth, she'd been lucky not to get caught by the neuro test station. She hadn't changed anything since her last tests, so she should come out looking as clean as ever.

The lab tech remained as annoying as her voice for the next four hours of tests. The worst of it wasn't the tests, it was keeping relatively drug-free for that long, when she wasn't even allowed access to her entertainment channel on her datapad. She couldn't complain though, since Jax was an Experimental. He'd get the same set of lab tests on every possible bodily extraction that she got, but he'd also get a much higher level of genetic manipulation than what she sought out illegally on that black market. He'd be a grumpy sod for the next few days as his body adapted to it all, a good time for her to slip off to Kendari.

Hours later, after a quick burger and beer, Kay shuttled down to Kendari. She started her visit as she always did—at a South Side salon that looked the same as all the other salons on this strip. She walked in with a small, black duffel bag over her shoulder. The usual styling chairs lined the two side walls in front of 3-D vid screens that were variously set to watch the stylist or sync to a personal datapad for uploading movies, news vids, or most any form of entertainment.

"Corporal Charlie!"

Kay turned in response to the fake name she'd used in most of her Kendari visits. Yasmin, the overweight shop owner waved Kay to the back of the shop.

"The usual," Kay said, taking a seat in front of Yasmin.

Yasmin ran her fingers through Kay's hair. "Tsh. You should have come a month ago." She lifted Kay's chin up and examined her eyes. "You give my shop a bad name, waiting this long. Look, I can see the blue showing through."

Kay shifted loose from Yasmin's grasp. "Couldn't get off work."

"Fine, fine. We'll dye your hair and eyes, but you'll stay for the full-body treatment this time. I have room for you in the private booth."

"Whatever you recommend." Anyone who knew Kay would know that was far too girlie for her, and they'd be right, but the appointment gave her reason to be in a private booth for over two hours.

In reality, she was in and out of the private booth within five minutes after her hair and eye dyes were done. The salon was a front for the genetics black market lab she frequented.

While the main Novan clans ensured their far-flung families got the best genetic upgrades, many of the lower castes had to make do with the government-sponsored baselines. That meant anyone willing to save up enough credit was looking for a black-market connection to bring them or their progeny a step up on the genetic-improvement ladder.

It all worked in Kay's favor as she stripped off her military fatigues in exchange for a set of civvies she kept in a paid-up locker in the Kendari shuttle port. As a product of the military, she had no "civvie" rights and no chance to wear the clothes in a legal sense. Just being caught in them would win her a ticket to the brig, but being caught in uniform in an illegal gene lab would get her in worse trouble.

She slipped out the back of the salon and down an access ramp to the sub-surface tunnels that wove through the fabric of the artificial planetoid's innards. The first tunnel maintained the quality and regulation expected from a formal installation, but after two quick turns, she pushed through a side hatch that should have been a utility closet. Instead, it led down another level and into a hodgepodge of poorly-lit access ways that would not have passed any safety check. But then, no government personnel came down this level, at least not on official business.

Five minutes later, she was in the lab and shuffled into another private booth. Names weren't exchanged here, only untraceable credits. She'd be here for a full two hours, getting treatments to enhance her reflexes, muscle conditioning, hearing, and most importantly, her vision. She paid the most for that, and was the real reason she doped her eyes black. The eye enhancements extended her vision to the full spectrum all Novans achieved, but it left telltale markers visible in her light blue irises. The black iris dye hid that. Contrary to what Valderrama thought, she didn't dye her hair and eyes to look more Novan, she dyed her eyes to cover her illegal treatments, and dyed her hair to avoid questions on why she changed her eye color to black.

A lab tech she'd seen on her last visit entered the booth. "Up on the table."

Kay stretched out on a flat gurney covered in plastic.

The tech hovered over her, attaching various instruments. "You'll need to rest after this."

"Yeah, I know." She'd be sore and have the mother of all headaches before she was done, but it would last her another three months. Whatever her next mission was, she should be back in plenty of time to visit Kendari again.

The tech poked the first needle into her arm, and Kay shut her eyes, bracing for the treatment to come.

CHAPTER 4

Gene Study—KDTU-02128 Originator Status-3050 AH

Project Troy, phase 3 Terran reintegration initiated. Next batch of 200 gene line originators altered for staggered release schedule from twenty-two prison camps. KDTU-02128 gene-mother modified based on profile gene identifications from stage 3 gene study. Additional sex orientation adaptations required to maximize modified gene line proliferation in the wild. Phase 3 tracking transferred to Nassien Research Division initiate Project Manager Benyan Nassien Halabi. Initial report for KDTU-02128 gene mother indicate successful reintegration at Buenos Aires Station (Terran).

Kay stood in formation with the rest of her platoon, one of four shipped out from New China. So far, they'd received minimal mission details, just as Halabi predicted. Someone was keeping a tight lid on wherever they were going. They'd spent five dreary weeks on an amphibious assault vessel that wasn't meant for long trips. Two hundred Marines bunked out in an emptied munitions bay didn't make for a comfortable trip. Nobody willing to talk had any mission details. The only thing Jax could uncover was that their rendezvous was in the middle of dead space with a massive naval transport ship. It wasn't until they docked and came aboard that they found out the name of the ship—the HMS Siria, a Latakia-class super transport. It had swallowed their ship and another material-support vessel that had loaded before them on the well deck. From the look of the deck, it could swallow at least two more ships.

Their company was lined up in the assembly deck, separated from the well deck by a five-meter wall of blast-proof alloy, in case of landing accidents. That didn't keep out the chill, though, and Kay wished she'd put on her uniform jacket instead of ramming it in her duffel bag. Platoon rank put them first in line and Kay stood to the right of Jax, with her duffel bag at her feet. Their C.O. and the other platoon commanders formed a short line perpendicular to hers, and two steps behind a grey-haired woman in captain's stripes, who stood next to the ship's XO, an overweight lieutenant commander in Navy blues, lost in the sea of Marine browns surrounding him. Kay hadn't been on many missions with their full company, but she recognized her captain's face from communications vids. From the size of their super transport ship and the expectant face of the XO, she guessed theirs wasn't the only company going on this mission.

The deck beneath her boots shook, announcing the arrival of another ship. All eyes turned to the vid-screens at the opposite end of the deck on her right that showed the activity in the well deck. A grey Class A Special Warfare ship slid into the well deck a half-kilometer away. The engines quieted to a low rumble and the deck settled. Kay didn't recognize the ship, but it wasn't a Marine vessel. Locked down laser cannons bulged from both port and starboard, with a short-range artillery array spread across the underbelly.

Jax let out a low curse. Kay shot him a quick glance, but his eyes were glued to the latest arrival. She looked back to study the ship. This time she noticed the telltale black stripe painted across the bow. That was a damned important detail Halabi left out.

They weren't alone in their shock. Her company captain took an involuntary step back from the vid-screen as the ship's hatch opened near the stern and lowered an access ramp with a metallic thud. For a minute, maybe two, there wasn't a sound on the deck except the hiss of the distant engine as it stopped completely. Then there was movement in the dark shadows of the open hatch. The rhythmic *clack, clack, clack* reached Kay's ears through the vid-screen speakers. Then she, and everyone else, saw the origin of that noise.

Two columns streamed out of the ship in double time, setting up a rhythm that Kay felt all the way up into her skull as they marched through the well deck hatch into the assembly deck, going from vid to real life giants. Squad after faceless squad in massive black exoskeletons formed by rank as one full company stretched from their ship to the farthest edge of Kay's company.

They were Black March troops. Thick black plate armor covered them from wide helmet to heavy boots. What looked like a uniform company of troops revealed subtle differences as they got closer. Sizes varied from larger than Jax to smaller than Ysabet. Some bore artillery across broad shoulders, while others had guns attached across their backs. All had rifles held at attention.

Kay could smell the scent change in everyone around her except Jax, the scent of fear. She knew her own scent was changing too, but that was plain old body odor. Jax would be all but pissing himself as he stared back at a full company of his worst nightmare. Kay wasn't too happy about their mission partners either, but she knew there was more to come. Halabi had told her that much, even if he'd left out the critical detail of a shared mission with the Black March.

Another moment of silence fell on the assembly deck and then, in perfect unison, the Black March company parted down the middle, forming a walled passageway reaching back to their ship. Eyes turned back to the vid screen as one lone female figure emerged from the darkness, fitted in a less-massive but more elaborate gray exoskeleton. Unlike the rest of her company, she left her helmet in the care of one of her two aides, who peeled off from the wall of honor and followed behind her like a pair of massive black deadly bodyguards. She marched slowly through the ranks of her own company, looking neither left nor right.

Details emerged as this woman entered the assembly deck. Her face was narrow, and the darkest of brown that spoke of an Old Earth African connection in her bloodline. Her eyebrows arched in perfect symmetry over black eyes that seemed to take in every detail, yet linger on no one. She wore the rank of lieutenant colonel with two differences, one subtle, one not. She had the crescent and star of her rank, but in red instead of silver, and strapped to her side was the ritual blade of the Nassiens.

This wasn't just any Nassien, this was a member of the ruling family, Nassien of Nassien, the only ones who wore those blades, shaped from the purest hardened synthetic obsidian to a razor edge shaper than any surgeon's scalpel.

The woman gave the XO a crisp salute. "Permission to come aboard."

"Lieutenant Commander Moki." The XO kept his eyes downcast as he saluted her. "Welcome aboard, Lieutenant Colonel Nassien."

She returned the salute. "Nassien Nomani, if you please. You have addressed the requirements for my troops?" Her voice was a rich contralto wrapped in the accent of the highest Novan caste.

"Apologies, Ser. Yes, their unique needs have been accounted for. They will be in the starboard berths on this deck. Ship's captain wishes to meet you as soon as possible to discuss logistics."

"Understood, Mister Moki. I shall see to my troops and then attend to your C.O." She brushed him aside with a wave of her hand and turned to Kay's captain. "We meet in my quarters at 13:00 hours. Bring your platoon commanders."

"Yes, ser." The captain's voice rang out louder than necessary, as she too kept her eyes downcast.

Kay barely registered the exchange. She was focused on Nassien's tantalizing scent. It was subtle in a way no other Novan woman's had been, but then Kay's exposure to the upper castes has never gone beyond Halabi. She hadn't realized she was staring until Jax's boot squeezed down on hers to bring her back to reality. She lowered her eyes, but not before Nassien registered her insult and took a step closer.

Even someone as loose with the rules as Kay knew you didn't look a Nassien in the eye. What was she thinking?

She wasn't, that was the problem. She let her libido take over. Now she stared at her boots and sweated it out as Nassien approached her company formation. Would she end up with that obsidian blade in her gut? A Nassien against a nameless grunt? No one would lift a finger to stop it except Jax, and he'd end up just as dead as she might be in a minute.

Head down and don't move, she told herself. She measured Nassien's approach in heavy footfalls and the increasing strength of her scent. It had changed, but not in a way that Kay recognized. She held her body poised to react and waited. If she were going to die, she'd take her gene line owner with her.

Nassien stopped directly in front of her with a hand on the obsidian blade hilt. Kay's mind sped up even without the Prilax as she took in the details of the grey exoskeleton. Nassien's body armor lacked the raw firepower obvious in the Black March. No shoulder launchers marred the smooth, grey exoskeleton, but the less-massive suit still had plate armor over the electro mechanics that guaranteed superior strength and speed. There was no obvious vulnerability, except the lack of a helmet. If the blade came out, she'd have to wrestle it from Nassien and slice across that exposed throat, all before the two hulking bodyguards took her out. Jax would react as soon as she did to block one of the guards. Ysabet on her right was an unknown. Would her crush on Kay drive her to suicide with the other hulk?

Nassien paused. Kay could imagine the confusion on her face even if she couldn't see it. Unlike Novans, Kay's pheromones didn't automatically sync in response to the approach of another Novan. Few had ever met a Terran face to face, so it took a moment or two before they realized they were facing an unaltered Terran and wouldn't get the expected response. If Nassien had pulled that knife first before pausing, the delay might have given Kay a slim advantage. No such luck for her. She clenched her jaw. *Do something, Damn it.*

Nassien studied Kay a moment longer, and then dropped her hand from her blade. "Let them pardon and forgive."

Kay's eyes shot up, but Nassien had already made a crisp military turn and was following the line of Kay's company back to the Black March. Kay didn't recognize what was obviously a quote, but she did know the language. Nassien said it in near-perfect Terran Standard, a language Kay had been forced to learn from the age of five. She stared until Nassien was swallowed up by the Black March as they marched to their berths.

Kay's C.O. signaled them to exit next. As they marched out, Valderrama elbowed past her. "She's going to gut you before the end of this mission." The grin on his face proved he hadn't a clue what Nassien had said to her. Likely no one in her company knew besides Jax, who was her language partner. She'd learned Terran Standard as Jax had learned the much more complex intricacies of Tarquin's top seven languages. Maybe languages were a gene-trait because he'd picked up nearly as much Terran as she had over the years.

She marched out with the rest of her platoon. She'd been damn lucky. Regardless of what her libido screamed, she'd have to keep as far away from Nassien as possible on this mission, whatever it was. Halabi could stuff his personal vendetta against this woman. Kay was going to mind her manners and survive whatever mess was coming their way.

"AYAAN MANJI NASSIEN Nomani," Ysabet read from her datapad as they sat in the noisy mess hall.

Jax sat on the opposite side of the table, stuffing food into his face. It took a lot of food to satisfy him. "Why the long name?"

"Her mission bio doesn't go into details, but I heard from

a guy in 2nd Platoon that her mother had an illicit affair with a Nomani. He says it caused a lot of trouble about twenty-three years ago. The Nomanis are a political caste, pretty far down from the top Nassiens."

Jax swallowed a mouthful. "You'd think she'd want to hide that instead of flaunt it by using both names."

Kay sat next to Ysabet, ignoring most of her meal. She resisted the urge to read Nassien's details over Ysabet's shoulder. She'd heard the same rumor, which meant there wasn't a lot of real information available on their resident royalty. She was more interested in what would come back from the Net crawl she sent off two hours ago from the ship's public com room. That would tell her more than any shipboard rumor mill, assuming the results came back in time. They had another day of acceleration before their ship reached a safe velocity to engage FTL drives. After that, they were in a communications black hole until they reached their mission destination, wherever that was.

Ysabet scanned more on her pad. "There's nothing here about the Black March."

Kay glanced at Jax, but the look on his face said he wasn't going to fill in the blanks for the kid. "They keep a low profile, adds to the mystique." Or dread fear, but Ysabet had been nervous enough lately.

Ysabet shoved her pad into her pocket. "Are they really suicide troops?"

"I don't think so. They get the special, high-profile missions." Kay left out the fact that there was a high mortality rate on any Black March mission.

"Have you seen any of them out of those big black suits?"

Jax clanked his fork down. "Some of them you won't ever see out of a suit. They are the genetic mistakes from gene lines like us. Some of them can't survive in normal conditions. That's why they have special berths. Those suits are mobile habitats for the worst of them."

Kay pushed the unappetizing mush around on her plate and

decided to change the topic before Jax blew up. "Any rumors on where this mission's going?"

Valderrama dropped his tray next to Jax and sat. "Won't matter to you, Terran." He shoved a fork full of gray mash into his mouth. "Our platoon's taking bets. I put a week's pay on you being dead before we arrive at mission coordinates."

Nice to be popular.

"Shut up, Valderrama." Ysabet was making a habit out of coming to Kay's rescue.

Valderrama spat a lump out onto his plate. "You screwing kids now, Terran?"

Kay flipped him off, but Ysabet didn't brush off the gibe so easily. She grabbed her tray and headed for the trash bin.

Jax slammed his tray on top of Valderrama's. "Do you have to be a jackass?" He went out after Ysabet.

Valderrama shook his head. "Maybe he's the one screwing the kid."

"Sex on a fire team is bad business." Kay stabbed at a lump of what might have been meat and rammed it in her mouth.

Valderrama shoved Jax's tray out of the way. "I knew the age difference wouldn't matter to you."

On that count he was wrong. The age did matter.

The food tasted like cardboard. Their mess hall, like everything else for their company, was last in line. Nassien and her company were top, followed by the Navy ship's crew. That left Kay's company with the smallest rack space, time-limited communal showers, barely-functional training compartments, and the worst food. The only taste of the high life they got was the communications compartment and the exercise compartment. Of that there were only two, one for the Navy, and one for everyone else.

She swallowed the lump of food in her mouth. "Field rations are better than this."

"Think of it as your last meal. Maybe it will be." He stabbed another lump and shoved it in his grinning face.

Someday, she'd pulverize that grin, or maybe cut him a

new one underneath, ear to ear. Not today, though. She had a Net crawl waiting for her. She got up and dumped her tray on his, just like Jax, and laughed at the stream of curses he hurled at her back as she walked out.

Their mess hall was on Deck 2 and the comm room was one deck down. She walked aft down the narrow passageway toward the stern of the ship and slid down the ladder well to Deck 3, where the Black March troops stayed. The comm compartment was on the port side of the ship so she had to walk through another two passageways. She paused at the second to let a senior officer pass, but otherwise managed not to encounter anyone but her own company and a couple of the crew.

She stepped through the open hatch. Communications had two cramped rows of public access terminals, all hooked into the ship's mainframe, and for another day, the interplanetary network. Three other members of her company were there, including Jax, huddled over his screen. She sat at a terminal farthest from the others, in a corner where no one could read over her shoulder.

Public access terminals didn't require a login, so what she pulled off the net couldn't be traced back to her. She navigated to the net crawl she'd triggered earlier and scanned the material. The results weren't as extensive as she'd thought they'd be. If she ignored the obvious PR sources, she only had a handful of articles. For coming from one of the highest Novan families, Nassien had left few traces of herself on the net.

Kay pulled up a PR article that linked to an image and scanned the contents. The picture showed Nassien kneeling in front of an elderly woman holding the obsidian blade. The article described some kind of coming-of-age ceremony. Nothing else of interest in that article except that she was an only child and her mother was a brigadier general. So much for the official news. Kay ignored the rest of the PR links and checked her first non government-sanctioned source.

The article was a scathing editorial on the privileges of caste. Nassien was one of three case studies used, and the article described her rapid rise through the lower officer ranks, suggesting she floated on family name rather than skill. Just what they all needed, an inexperienced officer leading their combined mission.

The next three articles proved useless, but the last article was wrapped in a security shell. Kay read the warning—any access to the host site would trigger an automatic trace back. She drummed her fingers on the console. Was it worth the risk? The article could be anything from illegal images to leaked classified documents. Could the trace back find her? It shouldn't. There was no login, no record of who was on this console. She considered the timing. Given their distances from the nearest base, it would take hours before the security trigger reached net security and initiated a trace back. By the time it round-tripped back, her ship would have hyper-jumped, and they'd be unreachable. She doubted anyone would bother to follow up on the trace back after her mission.

She opened the article. It was a classified document, but not from the military. Out of the corner of her eye she saw Jax get up and head her way. She scanned the article fast, trying to catch important keywords. With the security trigger, she couldn't go back and reread. Damned poor time for him to notice she was in the same compartment.

She shut down just as Jax put a hand on her shoulder. "We need to talk."

"This better be good." She pushed away from her console, not bothering to hide how ticked off she was at the interruption. That document had some choice topics. She'd only got two facts out of the document before she shut down—that Nassien's father was dead, and someone wanted Nassien dead too. She'd survived two assassination attempts. The document promised to detail the second attempt, but Kay didn't get the chance to read the details. No wonder Nassien had two personal bodyguards trailing her around the ship.

Jax didn't say a word as he led her up two decks and across the ship to the starboard training compartments. They passed navy crew who paused for Jax's superior rank, but he didn't acknowledge any of them. Whatever was on his mind, it left him little room for common ship courtesy. He picked an empty compartment and stepped in. Kay shut the hatch behind them. The training compartment was filled with blank simulator screens built into exam desks. They'd see plenty of use as soon as they hit the boring trip time through hyperspace. Even she'd want to log some sim time, just to break up the boredom.

Kay had her choice of empty seats but leaned against the bulkhead instead. "I gave up a good net crawl for this. Make it good."

Jax pulled out the nearest chair and sat. He powered up the desk and flipped on the first sim that came up. A holo image emerged from the desk and began the program. That would ensure enough background noise to block their conversation from any ship recorder.

He swiveled around in his seat to face away from the running sim. "I've been digging up info on our new friends."

"Friends?"

"The Black March."

To each his own obsession. "Learn anything interesting?"

"Some. We'll be cleaning up their droppings, whatever this mission is, but we knew that as soon as they marched in. Black March don't share missions, they take over. What's interesting is this is a newly-formed company with a new C.O. They'll be out to prove themselves."

"At our expense." Just what she wanted, a mystery mission with green troops.

"There's something else, something Halabi told me before we left."

Kay didn't flinch, but she glanced around the compartment on instinct before she got herself under control. "What did he say?"

Jax leaned in. "My gene line is here. One of the Black March is my gene line."

Shit. Jax's nightmare just came true, right in this screwed up mission. "Did he tell you who?"

"No, just that he's two generations from me and has a stronger Novan influence. It could be any one of them."

"So why'd he tell you?"

Jax looked away. "They don't put just any gene lines in Black March. It's the failures that go there, the terminated lines. I have no future."

"They haven't made you Black March, yet. Hell, this person, whoever he is, is far removed from your direct gene-set. He's more Novan by now than Tarquin. Who's to say they didn't just terminate that generation. They could spin another set off you."

"It doesn't matter. It's my genes, my family. We failed."

It was a dead-end argument. Jax believed what he assumed real Tarquins believe. Tarquins lived in close family structures, even more than Novans. He took personal responsibility for every bit of his DNA, wherever it got mixed. Kay didn't suffer from the same delusion. She had herself and she had Jax. Her mission was always the same. "Focus on staying alive, okay? That's what your long lost kin is doing if he has any sense."

"There's got to be something special about this mission, whatever it is. No one ever meets their gene line."

"Or maybe it's just Halabi's way of having fun." Had to be Halabi, but why? "Maybe if I could have finished that net crawl, I'd know more. All I learned was that Nassien has enemies, including Halabi."

"Halabi has enemies, too." Jax's expression was unreadable as he stood up to go, but his skin tone changes spoke for him. He was pissed.

"What now?" Kay didn't like his mood. Jax was the stable one. If he went off, there'd be some serious trouble for Halabi to clean up, if they survived.

"If there's any Tarquin left in this guy, I'll find him." He flipped off the sim and walked out the hatch.

Frigging Halabi. It had to be another one of his psych tests. Poke at their trigger points and watch the monkeys dance. He was jerking Jax around with this gene line connection and that just pissed her off. Maybe this time she'd give him the dance he was waiting for.

He said he'd clean up whatever mess she made, right? Maybe she needed to make one before Jax did.

SHIP TIME WAS the dullest part of Kay's life. The weeks, sometimes months, between destinations, meant filling the time with training, pre- and post-mission briefings, exercise, vids, and if she was lucky, sex. They weren't starting pre-mission briefings until they hit communications silence at hyper-jump speed. That left her with one thing on her mind, sex. Ignoring the Black March, she had the Navy and her own company to cruise. Plenty of options.

At 19:00 hours, she reported to the firing range to join the rest of her squad for some time-filler training. The shipboard firing range was set up on part of the assembly deck, since that had no use until they reached their destination. The far bulkhead was lined with electronic targets, each keyed to the individual firing cubicles set up in front of the nearside bulkhead to the right of the hatch Kay stepped through.

As the last one in, she had only a standard NV-17 multi-artillery assault rifle to practice with, not her weapon of choice. Jax and Ysabet were in side-by-side cubicles so Kay took the empty slot next to them and ignored Jax, the way he'd been ignoring her since their little Halabi chat. He had an NV-17 as well, but Ysabet was sighting down the barrel of an SR-29-AM, the top of the line anti-material rifle with an accuracy range over three kilometers in the right hands. Kay last used it to destroy the missile-guidance package on the mission that Yang never came back from.

She keyed her rifle into the cubicle so the target could track her accuracy. The weapons fired blanks, but the targets detected the projected range and marked off what would have been hits with real bullets. She fired off a full clip in automatic mode, tearing through her target but registering a mediocre accuracy score. She took her next clip in manual and switched the target screen to a series of humanoid shapes. She picked away at the vitals on each of her next targets, bringing her score back up to its normal accuracy.

As she loaded her next clip, she caught a glimpse of Ysabet's accuracy score and cringed. A beautiful weapon like that deserved a better handler. She put down her weapon, shut down her range, and walked around the partition that separated her from Ysabet, an act that immediately shut down Ysabet's range, for safety.

"Hi." Ysabet lowered her rifle.

Kay turned the range back on. "Show me how you're sighting your targets."

Ysabet shouldered her rifle and fired a hit on her next target, taking out the center of a Terran radar dish.

"Go for another target."

This time Ysabet blew the front windscreen off a truck.

Kay saw the problem. "Your sighting is fine but it's just like targeting a human. Dead center isn't always the sweet spot when you're taking out equipment."

She pulled up the next target, a comm tower with three cones at the top and a power box on the lower right. "How would you take this one out?"

"Three fast shots, one for each cone."

Kay shook her head. "You're making it too hard. Look for the quick kill."

Ysabet studied the target. "The power box."

"Right. One hit takes all three cones out. Always know where the brain is, where to take that one shot that will cripple the equipment."

Ysabet studied her next three targets and hit the kill spot in one shot each time.

"Good. You want to study up target types so you know where the brain is on each type without having to think about it."

Ysabet took out the next two targets with better speed and accuracy.

Kay threw an arm around her shoulder. "Almost better than sex, isn't it?"

Ysabet fumbled with her rifle. "Almost."

Ysabet's reaction was predictable but Kay was slow to drop her arm. Still, sex on a fire team—bad idea. She backed off a step. "Log out one of the target manuals for this gun. You want to know on instinct where that sweet spot is."

She checked her rifle back in and left the range double-time. If she didn't find some kind of relief for her libido, she'd do something stupid. She opted to leave the kid with Jax, since he'd taken on the big brother role lately. The two of them disappeared for hours at a time. If she didn't know it was biologically impossible, she'd swear they were doing it somewhere.

She needed to be doing it somewhere herself. There weren't a lot of places on the ship where people congregated. She had the choice of mess hall or one of the exercise compartments. She climbed up a Deck 1 ladder where the ship's crew bunked and headed for the enlisted and noncommissioned officer gym. A random pickup or a workout—either one would help her out at this point.

The gym was busy with a mix of ship's crew and Marines, none of whom she recognized at first glance. The gym held the standard weight training and cardio equipment, along with large mats for self-defense classes. With most of the equipment busy, she grabbed a practice knife and headed for the mats where a hand-to-hand competition was starting up. Most of the participants were Marines, stripped down to tan tank tops and boxers, but a couple of Navy personnel participated as well.

One crewmate watched her approach, a short woman with curly black hair in navy tank and shorts, and gave her an obvious appraising stare.

Kay returned the appraisal, taking in a tone body, well-endowed in the important regions. She stepped in next to her and sensed the woman's pheromone shift. Yeah, sex wasn't going to be such an elusive target on this ship after all.

CHAPTER 5

Gene Study—KDTU-02128 Replicant Status-3050 AH

Detailed analysis of Crèche D gene set verification proved replicants have been genetically compromised. Full termination required and all gene study results purged. Project review determined Crèche D replicants cloned from post-modification gene-mother stem cells. Emergency funding approved for replacement replicants with the creation of Crèche E. First-batch replicants tested to verify pure unaltered Terran status before proceeding to term with six viable embryos.

Fourth-stage preliminary funding delayed.

The *Siria* transitioned to hyper-jump speed in the early morning hours, ship time. Kay was in her rack less than an hour when she felt the telltale nauseous disorientation that occurred when a ship broke the hyper-jump barrier. She curled into a ball and focused on keeping her last meal down. If she hadn't hooked up with that crewmate, she might have slept through the transition like the rest of her squad, though it hit her worse than any Novan. She wondered if there was a gene manipulation for space travel as well? If she ever managed to save some spare credits, she might have to check that enhancement out with her black market contacts.

She waited for her stomach to feel more like it was inside her body rather than out. It took longer than normal, thanks to too much beer and not enough sleep. By the time she felt human again, the rest of her squad were rolling out of their racks for breakfast. She stayed in her rack. Food was less of a need than sleep.

She didn't know how much later it was when Ysabet shook her awake.

"Come on. We're finally going to hear about this mission."

Kay groaned into her pillow. "How much time do I have?"

"Ten minutes."

Ysabet stepped back as Kay dropped out of her rack. She was awake enough now to feel the bruises from a night of hand-to-hand combat competition. It gave her the ability to vent some frustration as well as a good stream of hookup options. Even the especially painful bruise where her opponent landed a solid hit on her jaw was worth it, though she'd be on soft rations for the day at least.

Kay yanked her tank top up and gave it a whiff. It passed the sniff test. "Who's giving the mission brief?" If it was their C.O. she could get away with putting back on yesterday's fatigues.

"It's a joint briefing with both companies."

That meant top brass and no day-old wrinkled clothes. Kay opened her locker, pulled out a clean set of fatigues, and got dressed, while Ysabet unsuccessfully tried to look like she wasn't watching the whole show.

Kay was tempted to ask Ysabet what Jax was up to, but opted against being nosey. "I need to hit the head."

Ysabet waited for her to emerge, and they rushed down to the unaltered aft section of the Deck 3 assembly area. The firing range was empty, but the rest of the deck was already packed with Marines on her left and Black March to her right. Both companies lined up by platoon to face an empty podium in the front.

She and Ysabet joined their squad in the front left. Showing up together was becoming their thing on this mission. Valderrama gave his usual snort of greeting but didn't bother to voice the obvious gibe about screwing the kid.

Jax stepped aside as Kay slipped in line between him and Valderrama. "Cutting it close."

Kay polished her scuffed boot on the back of her pants. "Late night." Just like he had, if his empty bunk was any indication. Were there any female Tarquins in those Black March troops?

She pulled her fingers through her short-cropped hair, as close to a comb as it would get today. She scanned the assembled Black March troops to her right. They didn't wear fatigues like her company of Marines but at least they weren't all in their rigid exoskeletons either. Those who could live without them wore black uniforms with no rank or insignia on any but the platoon commanders who stood at the front in mirror formation to the Marine platoon commanders. From the variety of faces and body types, they must represent genetics from every known sentient bipedal species. There was at least one Chankran in the command ranks, from the blocky body type of their high-gravity home planet. There was also an Aquaran with reddish-brown kelp hair, and a possible Novan-Chameleon blend. She couldn't see any obvious Tarquin women, at least not with the deep red skin that Jax had.

The hatch slammed open, and Nassien marched in with her two bodyguards. Her black hair was pulled back into the same tight bun that emphasized her high cheekbones. She had the same black uniform as her troops, with her rank stitched to the collar. Her two trailing guards wore Marine brown with the stripes of sergeants. So they weren't Black March after all, regardless of the exoskeletons they wore on arrival.

Nassien stepped up to the front podium and flicked on the holo display. The far bulkhead disappeared in favor of a 3-D view of a multi-planet system. "This is Chagos. The system has five planets and seven gas giants. Our interest is the second and third planets. The second planet is our primary source for rare earth-heavy metals, including monazite, the stuff that fires our laser cannons and provides the flexible strength for our space fleet. That's not our target. The third planet is the reason this mission has been handled with the highest security. It houses one of three backup gene banks. The entire Novan genome in its current version as well as every variant for the last one-hundred-and-thirty years is stored there."

A hush fell over the assembly. The gene bank locations were a highly-protected secret. Kay stared at the nondescript dot and knew if she did a net crawl on Chagos, it wouldn't show up. It probably wasn't even the real name. Nassien wouldn't trust this many soldiers with that information. Likely only the ship's navigator knew for sure where their destination was compared to known space.

"Six weeks ago, Intel brought us details of a Terran invasion plan for these coordinates."

Kay didn't care about the gene bank but most everyone around her did, besides Jax. Even the Black March had eyes glued to the holo display. She wondered if their genetic makeup was considered official Novan variants. Looking at the hodgepodge of cross-species faces, she doubted it.

"We don't know if the Terrans are aware of the gene bank or not, but if we realign all in-system resources as a precaution to protect that gene bank, the Terrans will definitely take notice." The holo zoomed into the third planet. The nondescript mass clarified into a planet with significant polar ice. The holo hovered over the mountainous southern landmass, just visible beyond the edge of the southern polar ice cap.

"The planet and gene bank have significant hidden defensive capabilities, but we don't know the size or capabilities of the Terran attack fleet. The government decided on this special ops mission as an added safety net. We are part of a joint task force responsible for reinforcing this planet's strategic sites." The halo zoomed in further, but Kay couldn't detect much besides mountains and snow. "My company will cover the main gene bank facility. We have sufficient force to repel any attempted Terran attack. The Marine company will remain in reserve to back up the inner-system defenses in case the Terrans go after the monazite mines instead."

The assembled Marine company shifted from silence to a low rumble of mutters that Kay joined in. "Reserves? We're spending an eternity in transit just to sit and do nothing when we get to Chagos?" That wasn't a job for Marines, that was for standard Army grunts. They wouldn't even get active duty pay at this rate. She glared at the Black March troops, but they remained quiet and in perfect formation. Genetic mutant bastards.

Nassien slapped the side of her leg in stony silence until the murmurs settled down. It took some heavy stares from Kay's platoon commanders, but eventually the deck was quiet enough for Nassien to continue. "Mission details are strictly need-to-know. Your platoon commanders have been briefed for their roles. Dismissed."

"That's it?" Valderrama grumbled. "I should have stayed in the mess hall."

Whatever grand ideas Halabi had for her making Nassien look bad went right out the airlock with that dismissal. Their entire company was being sidelined. Kay could spend the rest of the mission in a drug-coma and it wouldn't matter. Given how dull this was going to be, and all for nothing, she just might do that.

The Black March troops stayed in formation while the Marines marched out, in less than regulation silence. Kay glanced back at the podium, but Nassien had already been swallowed up by her bodyguards.

THEIR DAYS CHURNED on in dull monotony, with nothing to do and nothing to look forward to. A few fights had already broken out between the Marines and Black March. Kay's platoon took to traveling together as much as possible, for protection. Of course that meant more time with Valderrama than was healthy for either of them.

"You want to know why we're ballast on this ship? The answer's right here." Valderrama jabbed a finger in Kay's direction as they walked to their mess hall on Deck 2. "No one's going to let a damned Terran traitor near the gene bank."

He wasn't speaking to her or Ysabet who walked beside her, and Jax had heard it enough in the past few days that he was skipping lunch today. No, Valderrama was just repeating his tirade for the benefit anyone else within hearing range. Even Ysabet was too distracted to bother with her usual comeback in Kay's defense. The kid was a bundle of nerves lately, and even the extra coaching time spent with Jax wasn't helping settle her down. Kay couldn't muster up the effort to care, either. She'd broken into her pharmacy early and was riding easy on a two day high.

The line building in the passageway toward the mess came to a slow halt. Either the entire company had showed up at once, or something was up. The one drawback to Kay's drug of choice was it made her extra hungry. Food delays weren't a good option.

"What's the holdup?" she said.

The Marines in front started moving backward. Valderrama grabbed the news out of one Marine as he passed them. "Kitchen fire. We've got to share the Deck 3 mess with the freaks."

Ysabet turned and ran back the way they'd come, pushing her way through the rest. And Kay thought she was the hungry one.

"What's your rush? The Black March can't eat all the food before we get there," Kay said, watching Ysabet race ahead.

"Yeah but half our company's probably there already, eating up any extras." Valderrama muscled his way forward.

One extra grumble from her stomach was enough to make Kay follow in his footsteps. He wasn't a tall man, but he was wide and solid and cut a determined path through the passageway to the ladder well leading down to Deck 3, where the Black March stayed. She hit the bottom of the ladder and the tail end of a short lunch line outside the mess hall. So much for avoiding the rush. Kay leaned against the bulkhead and waited, Valderrama at her elbow.

"What was that?" he asked.

"What?"

"Useless Terran hearing. Sounded like a bang."

Kay heard the second bang as a blast of smoky air flattened her against the bulkhead. She and everyone else dropped to the deck. Her ears popped from the pressure change after the second and third explosion.

A tense stillness followed, but no fourth explosion occurred. The air smelled of smoke and fire-fighting chemicals as Kay did a quick body-check pat down before she got off the deck. Other than the ringing in her ears, she was unhurt. A quick scan around her showed everyone else in the passageway was okay as well, but the screams of pain from the mess hall in front of them said the rest weren't so lucky.

Valderrama was back on his feet first.

Kay pushed up next to him, fighting the lethargy of her two-day high. "What's the rush?"

"Ysabet." He scanned over the heads of those still on the ground. "I don't see her in the passageway in front of us." Valderrama stepped over the mess hall threshold with Kay at his heels. They had the perfect hate-hate relationship, but that didn't extend to the rest of their fire team.

The smoky air was worse in the mess hall. Kay covered her mouth and nose with her shirt as she scanned the area. Fire-fighting foam coated most of the tabletops, or what was left of them closer to the center of the mess hall. The blast radius from two separate explosions was obvious from the spread of debris and bloody bodies. The humanoid damage dwindled down to major, then minor injuries and finally, the healthy ones who were already working through the debris to look for survivors.

Kay and Valderrama started with the nearest blast section. This had the highest concentration of Marine uniforms. Of course a mess hall full of Marines and Black March would segregate into their own turfs. Kay scanned to the left while Valderrama scanned to the right. It was easy to discard the dead and dying. They were bleeding from multiple cuts from what looked like shattered glass. None were small enough in stature to be Ysabet.

Valderrama picked the unusual pieces of debris out of one of the Marine's body. He held a couple of razor-sharp glass or plastic shards, one of which cut into his finger as he examined it. "This is home-brew shit." He dropped the shards and scanned the mess hall. "Not good."

Kay trusted that her fire team explosives expert knew what he was talking about. Certainly other experts from other squads, Marine and Black March, had to be noticing the same thing. Kay followed Valderrama's gaze to the far right. That section had its scattering of the dead and wounded, but further away from the two obvious blast areas. Worse, it was the only place where the Black March and Marine survivors mingled at all, and the voices were getting louder. Valderrama headed into the thick of it, but Kay wasn't interested in group dynamics at this point. Let the M.P.s deal with it, when they got here.

Where was Ysabet?

She glanced at the area where two blast zones overlapped and picked the area with the most Marine uniforms. This group had a few Black March mixed in, those closest to the overlap were just as dead as the Marines. As for survivors, the injured were looked after exclusively by their own kind.

Kay stepped over bodies as she made her way through the mess. She kept her face covered now more for the smell than the smoke. She spotted one dead Marine amongst three Black March bodies. The Marine body was half buried under the remnants of a collapsed table. It was hard to gauge size from just the legs and half torso view, but it wasn't a big Marine under there.

Kay stood in front of those legs, but her feet felt glued to the deck. The kid survived her first active mission. She couldn't be dead from some freak mess hall brawl. Even as the thought flickered and died, she knew it was possible. There weren't that many small Marines in their company. The universe really could be just that sucky a place.

"Terran!"

Kay looked up on instinct when Valderrama bellowed that label at her across the mess hall. He was in a cluster of Black March troops surrounding a relatively unaffected area of the mess hall. It had a few bodies, but wasn't a bomb site that she could tell.

He waved her over. Kay took one last look at the body under the table. If it were Ysabet, she'd still be there later and just as dead. Kay stepped over the legs and walked toward Valderrama's group. Had the mess hall gotten just that little bit quieter?

As she approached the group, Valderrama stepped aside and pointed down. The body was unmistakable. From the back, Ysabet looked like she'd just curled up for a nap, but the front told a different story. Hundreds of those tiny bomb shards tore up her front, leaving a burned, bloody mess. Kay looked away. Even for a veteran, it was an ugly death to witness. Ysabet was the third blast zone.

"Terran."

Great, others were now using Valderrama's label for her. Kay glanced at one of the Black March surrounding Ysabet's body. He was a lanky black-clad soldier with a fuzz of red hair and sunburned skin. He jabbed his thumb back at Ysabet. "She's one of yours and she was on top of the third bomb."

One bomb in each dining area of the mess hall. The pattern made more sense now, but why Ysabet? "Maybe she tried to diffuse it."

"Maybe she set it," the soldier said, his deep brown eyes never leaving Kay's face.

Valderrama clenched his fists. "She was just a kid."

The mood around Kay was shifting and not in a good way. Marine faced Black March, and she wanted out of this showdown, fast. "It doesn't matter anymore. She's dead, so let the M.P.s figure it out when they get here. We should be helping the survivors, not playing detective." She turned away.

The Black March soldier stepped in her way. "Maybe she had help. Your teammate called you Terran."

Fucking Valderrama. She stared up at the redheaded soldier. It took her a moment to recognize his skin wasn't burned, but reflected the remnants of Tarquin genes in his genetic background. Mixing and matching genes like kids with finger paints, that's what the Novans did, and the entire Black March were their masterpieces.

"I'm a genetic experiment, just like you," she said. A second later, his fist slammed into her gut. She twisted away from the punch, but not soon enough to deflect much of the blow. She doubled over, gasping for breath. The son of a bitch sucker-punched her.

CHAPTER 6

Gene Study—KDTU-02128 Originator Status—3058 AH

Project Troy, Phase 3—Full reintegration achieved. Limited local-access monitoring available but no signs of rejection noted for any originators. Birth records show enhanced fertility procedures successful in first years, with average of 2.4 offspring, an increase of 28% over phase 1 and 2 Troy reintegration from 3030 AH and 3040 AH. Project continues to utilize passive monitoring, limited to gene line originators only, to ensure stability and acceptance. All resultant offspring to be placed on priority 2 tracking. Non-viable originators (no offspring in first five years) removed from project monitoring to reduce project expenditures. Tracking also terminated for second-generation offspring from phase 1 after initial tracking from 3048 - 3055 AH. Proliferation in the wild determined successful. Funding approved for Phase 4 reintegration based on acceptable gene line approvals from target originators.

The Black March soldier grabbed Kay's shirt to aim the next punch, but she came up on her own speed and whammed a double-fist to his groin. It was his turn to double over. She balanced on the balls of her feet, ready for his next move after landing that good hit. Her victory was short-lived—another set of hands grabbed her from behind. So much for a fair fight.

She had just enough time to see Valderrama off to her right, making no attempt to help her, before the volley of pain began. The redhead punched her in the jaw and then another to the gut. She couldn't see the asshole holding her from behind. She landed one hard-booted kick to his calf, but not with enough power to loosen his hold on her.

Another Black March joined the fun and landed an unopposed fist to her face that had her spitting blood. They turned her into a punching bag, but not for long. Her multiple opponents turned into just the original two as the mess hall broke out into a full riot between Marine and Black March. She squirmed one arm free and blocked his next swing at her, then tried to leg-sweep him, but he was too quick for her. She landed a few kicks but nothing slowed him up until a bigger, redder fist landed its first blow across his temple.

Jax had shown up.

Kay twisted out of the hands of the chickenshit that held her for the punching-bag routine. It was another Black March soldier of indiscriminate genetic makeup. Not that it mattered. Pain was pain and Kay had a lifetime of experience taking it and giving it back. She had plenty to give back now, and she gave it back in full, running on adrenaline and fight instinct. She landed punch after punch until another set of hands pulled her off the bloodied soldier.

"Stand down."

The voice didn't register. Kay twisted out of the grip of her latest captor and landed a solid shot to his solar plexus before he threw her to the ground and pinned her down.

"Stand down, soldier!"

This time the voice registered. Nassien. Kay's face was plastered to the deck so the only view she had was of a pair of blood-smeared boots. If that was Nassien, she'd seen some action of her own.

Kay relaxed as much as she could with the massive body pressing down on top of her. His brown-clad arm pushed her head into the deck. It was one of Nassien's own bodyguards. How lucky could she get?

The thrill of the fight wore off. Her right eye was swollen shut, she couldn't take in a full breath without extreme pain, and her jaw ached. The rest of her body hurt, but those were the top ones. She could hear soldiers shuffling into some kind of formation behind her. Party's over.

"Let her up."

The body pinning her let go. Kay was slower to get up. The problem with riots was once the fun ended, you had days of pain ahead. Kay felt more damage which she couldn't localize into individual points of pain, and the remnants of her high wasn't dampening much of it. She got up on one knee and tried to stand. A sharp stab in her chest brought her back to her on her knees.

"Shit." That punching-bag episode broke at least one rib.

"Can you walk?" Nassien asked.

Kay avoided eye contact. She was at least that aware of her situation. She tried standing, again, but the pain was too much. More than one broken rib. "No, ser."

Nassien turned to the crowd. "Are any other members of her squad here?" Jax and Valderrama stepped forward. "Carry her to the brig."

Not to a medic? Asshole. Pain laced her side as they hoisted her up. She glared at Nassien, protocol be damned. The woman didn't give her a second glance as she ordered a handful of others to the brig as well, including Jax and Valderrama. Jax looked ready to explode, but Valderrama just looked sore. Good. She hoped the bastard got a good beating from it all.

It was a long, painful slog to the brig. Maneuvering the ladder up a deck was the worst of it. She cursed Nassien's name on every step up. She had to pause on the next deck before she blacked out. A handful of Marines eased past them, but no Black March. So much for fair and unbiased leadership.

They were the last to reach the brig. Jax helped her through the hatch, where they checked in with the officer on duty. Black barred cells lined both sides of the narrow beige passageway. There were too many Marines to pack into the small number of cells. She and Jax took one cell, booting Valderrama to share a cell with another Marine.

Kay sank down on the sole bunk and tried not to breathe too deeply. "Ysabet's dead."

Jax didn't reply. He was a red cloud of anger pacing the short length of the bunk, from bars to small but functional head. Step, step, turn. Step, step, turn. Kay eased back on the bunk and closed her one good eye against the solitary overhead light recessed into a protective cage. She tried to recapture her earlier high, but it wasn't happening. She was a battered wreck. And Jax was an explosion waiting to happen.

"She's dead." Kay wasn't going to lose that last image of the kid for a long time. "What the hell was she doing on top of that last bomb?"

Jax squatted down, his head in his hands. "She was too young to be part of this mission. It's all wrong."

The bars to their cell slammed open, cutting short their first attempt at conversation in a week. Finally, a medic from ship's personnel. She carried a sizable black bag and wore light blue disposable scrubs that were already bloodstained but she didn't stop to change.

"What are your injuries?"

"Ribs mostly," Kay said. "And the obvious facial reconstruction."

The medic pulled on fresh gloves and examined Kay's eye first, then moved Kay's jaw back and forth with all the tenderness of a stone wall.

"No permanent damage." The medic pulled two cold packs out of her bag and tossed them on the bunk.

The medic rolled up Kay's sleeve and jabbed it with a needle.

Kay winced. "What's that for?"

"Standard blood work." She slipped the blood sample into a portable analysis kit. Within seconds, she gave Kay a raised eyebrow, but otherwise said nothing about the drugs still lingering in Kay's system. It wouldn't be the first time she'd been caught high. The medic moved her attention to Kay's ribs. She clamped her jaw shut to hold back a scream.

"Hmm." The medic took out a hypo spray of pain meds and jabbed Kay in the arm. "The shirt needs to come off."

She pushed Kay up to a sitting position and helped her out of the shirt. Lifting the tank top up exposed an area already dark with bruising. The medic pulled out a portable scanner and ran it over Kay's exposed chest.

"Two clean breaks. No threat to your lungs."

She pulled a brown roll of bandaging out of her bag and wrapped Kay's ribs. Tears floated in Kay's one open eye. Broken ribs were one of the most painful side effects of a good brawl.

"Don't do anything else stupid and you'll live." The medic packed up her equipment and took off, leaving Jax to help Kay back into her shirt.

"Not paid for her bedside manner, is she?" Kay said as she lay back on the bunk. Between the pain meds and wrapped ribs, she was feeling better, not too bad, overall, for an ex-punching bag.

Jax sat on the edge of the bunk. "She's been busy."

Kay remembered the number of wounded before the brawl, and worse, the number of dead. "We're going to be short on this mission."

"We weren't a part of this mission anyway, remember?"

She hadn't remembered, but he was right. They were still just ballast, another reason Ysabet shouldn't be dead. "Why'd she do it?"

"Who did what? Nassien? Because we're meaningless to them, disposable. That's what they do, you know, just throw Black March against impossible odds. If they all die, so what? If some of them live, they don't get the praise, only the C.O.s like Nassien get anything out of it all. It's not right, you know."

She was asking about Ysabet, not Nassien, but didn't stop Jax's tirade. At least he was talking to her again. It wouldn't help to know why Ysabet did it anyway. Dead was dead. She fought back against that last image of Ysabet playing against the back of her closed eyes and sank into the mental numbness of the pain meds.

KAY STOOD IN the passageway outside Nassien's quarters, waiting for her turn at the interrogation grill. They'd spent less than a shift in the brig before being put on cleanup duty. The mess hadn't suffered much physical damage, but there had been two other sites hit on the ship. Their Marine transport was crippled, which seemed a waste since they weren't participating in the mission at this point anyway. The final bomb decimated one of the special Black March bunk sections, but the Marines weren't allowed in there to help with cleanup. After this attack, Kay doubted anyone would let the two companies anywhere near each other. Of the hundred Black March troops, less than seventy remained, whereas the Marines suffered only seven fatalities, including Ysabet.

Jax emerged from Nassien's quarters. His jaw still had the clenched look that was a permanent fixture since the explosion, but his eyes betrayed a sense of confusion.

"Anything I should know about before I go in there?" Kay asked.

"I don't know. She's fishing for conspirators, and I think you, Valderrama, and me are at the top of her list, because of Ysabet. They don't have any other details about who created the bombs, or why those targets."

"So it's a witch hunt, great." Being the lone Terran made her a favorite scapegoat. She just might end up taking up permanent residence in the brig.

"I don't know. She's let me out of the brig."

The hatch opened behind Jax before he had a chance to finish. One of Nassien's bodyguards stepped out and took up position outside the closed hatch. Jax gave Kay a pat on the shoulder and left her to wait it out on her own. She eyed up the bodyguard but couldn't tell if he was the one who'd flattened her to the deck or not. He wore the same brown uniform, but with more obvious armament now. He had a pistol strapped to his thigh, but the gun that caught Kay's attention was the SX-21 automatic rifle he held across his chest. This guy meant business.

A few minutes later, he opened the hatch and waved her in. The dark look he gave her then said this was the one she'd gotten a good punch in before being tackled. Kay stepped through and the bodyguard sealed the hatch behind her.

Rumor had it that Nassien's personal assistant died in the bunk explosion, and one bodyguard was in sickbay. So it was just Kay and the other bodyguard so far. Nassien's quarters were tight, but then all ship space was limited. There were two side hatches leading off from what was obviously Nassien's office. A slab of a desk with a net console and a chair dominated the office. No other furniture or decoration existed in the Spartan area. Kay wasn't going to be sitting, then.

Nassien wasn't in the front office but her scent permeated the air even over the two male pheromone scents. The bodyguard opened the second side hatch and stepped back to wait. Kay stared at what she'd never seen before on a military ship, a prayer compartment.

She caught a glimpse of Nassien's dark hands rolling up the edge of a rug that was set at an odd angle to the hatch, and hanging from a bulkhead bolt was the complex Mecca clock that tracked both time and direction in deep space. Kay had seen religious areas set aside before on civilian ships, but never on a military vessel. It didn't belong here. Novan Military kept a strict separation from all religions after the wars of 2850 AH. Guess that didn't apply to those at the top, but it might explain the non-regulation red color of Nassien's star and crescent rank insignia. It must have religious significance.

Kay stood for another five minutes before Nassien finished and entered the main compartment. The bodyguard sealed the prayer compartment hatch, and then stood mute as a statue. Nassien never glanced her way as she sat, but Kay slapped to attention on instinct, ignoring the twinge in her still-aching ribs.

Nassien's unique pheromones washed over her again, and her reaction was hard to stifle. She'd be hunting down a release for that after this meeting, if she were let free from the brig as well. And if her ribs could handle it. Meanwhile, she kept her expression neutral, stared at the desktop, and waited.

"At ease." Nassien slid into her chair with a graceful, fluid motion and typed something into her console.

Kay stood with her hands behind her back, wishing she'd had some inkling of what Nassien's goals were for this interrogation, because she had no illusions this was anything other than a grilling about the explosion and riots. She could tell Nassien she was just in the wrong place at the wrong time, not that anyone would believe her besides Jax.

Whatever came up on the console caught Nassien's attention, and she looked up at Kay. "So you are the one at the center of this mess."

Once again, Nassien switched to Terran standard. Kay kept her eyes on the desk and negated the claim, in Novan.

"When I speak to you in Terran, answer me in Terran."

Kay grasped for a Terran-standard equivalent to the gender-neutral ser, but came up empty. "Yes . . . Ma'am."

"The charge against you is for striking a superior officer and inciting a riot, and this according to your own squad mate. Do you accept this charge?"

Someday, she would kill Valderrama. "No, Ma'am, I do not. I was struck by one of your soldiers. In the act of defending myself, I may have hit my attacker."

"May have? You broke my company commander's nose."

Kay resisted the urge to grin. She didn't remember landing a good one on the redheaded bastard. Commander, though? Why didn't the damned Black March use rank insignia like every other branch of the military did? "My attackers did not bear the rank of commander, Ma'am, or any rank insignia. I fought with a red-headed man, a Tarquin mix." What kind of bullshit story did Valderrama tell?

"Correct on both accounts. Commander Tajex received his field promotion after the riot. And he's from the same gene line as one of the other surviving members of your fire team, I believe he abbreviated his gene line designation to Jax."

What a great time for Jax's long-lost cousin to show up. She wondered if Jax knew he beat the crap out of his own gene line.

"And you are?"

"KDTU-02128, 4th Stage, Crèche H, Ma'am."

Nassien flicked an impatient hand at her console. "That I can see, soldier. What do you call yourself?"

"Kay Deetchu." Kay resisted the urge to glare at Nassien. Since when did officers care what their experimental rats called themselves? That and the insistence on conversing in Terran Standard grated on her nerves.

"Interesting adaptations you all make. Anyway, Commander Tajex confirms your story. Those charges will be dropped." Nassien typed something on her console then looked up again. "You should reevaluate your relationship with your remaining fire team. Such misunderstandings can lead to critical incompatibilities over time."

Kay was going to bust an incompatible bat over Valderrama's head for this.

Nassien leaned back in her chair. "What of your involvement in the attack on my company?"

Her company? "Ma'am, there were seven casualties and thirteen serious injuries to the Marines, as well as the destruction of our transport vessel." Not to mention her own broken ribs and bruised jaw.

"Yes," Nassien said. "And twenty-one Black March deaths, with an additional forty-two injured, over half of which will not be functional in time for this mission. Your gene line is known for its tactical capabilities. Analyze the evidence and tell me where it leads you."

Kay was about to give a glib response, but resisted the urge. She didn't like that Nassien bothered to do a deep read into her record. Most C.O.'s ignored the gene line connection and left her alone as just another grunt. That's what she was here for right? To blend in, be a grunt, and see what magic her gene line produced that the Nassien geneticists could bastardize for their own enhancement programs.

She didn't have Jax to hide behind here, and Nassien wasn't letting her loose any time soon. Frowning at the deck, she pulled together everything she'd heard about, from Nassien and what she'd seen during her cleanup duty. Something didn't fit. If it was a few Marines with a grudge against the Black March, why take out the Marine transport as well, especially when they'd already been grounded. And why was a kid like Ysabet involved?

What did suddenly fit into place didn't make her feel any more comfortable about her own skin. Kay lifted her eyes as far as Nassien's hands resting on her console touch screen. "Someone wants you to fail, Ma'am."

Halabi, obviously. But who else had he enlisted? Jax was too by-the-book, and he wouldn't risk his own gene line in the attack, even if he didn't know which one was Tajex at the time. And there was too much planning involved to say Ysabet went off the edge on her own.

Nassien steepled her fingers under her chin. "Explain."

"The mess hall attack was directed at the Black March. It was a last-minute change that Marines were even present. That suggests the Black March were the primary targets, given that the other main target was the Black March bunk space. If that explosion there used the same shrapnel base, it was set for maximum physical injury instead of property destruction."

"It wasn't," Nassien said. "The bunk space was a specialized habitat that catered to the unique environmental needs of some of my troops. The explosion took out those environmental controls, leading to the outright death of twelve and harming another fifteen before they could access their suits."

"That suggests a personal grudge of some kind, Ma'am." That was close to the truth if Halabi was involved, but did Nassien recognize it?

"Personal grudge?"

"The same kind of bombs used in the mess hall could have been deployed in any of the Black March bunks, but someone took the effort to switch tactics and go for the environmentals. You change tactics for a reason."

Nassien nodded. "The reason being then someone hated the specials."

That was the first time Kay had heard anyone use that term to reference the real genetic mutants in the Black March, the mistakes.

"So far your explanation doesn't eliminate the obvious option that this was a Marine attack on my troops."

"Respectfully, Ma'am, it does. The personal grudge against the . . . specials suggests a deeper knowledge of the individual Black March platoons than the average Marine is aware of, suggesting a Black March origin for that attack. As for the Marine transport's destruction, it removes the possibility of the Marine company filling in for the decimated Black March company. Combine that with the compromising death of my fire team member, and it suggests Marine involvement as well." No sense tiptoeing around the obvious about Ysabet. Kay would kill whichever bastard had brainwashed that kid. Sloppy planning by someone. "The two groups don't exactly get along well, so it has to be a third party pulling the strings."

"Interesting synopsis." Nassien leaned forward, elbows on her desk. "And where does this leave you?"

Was it getting hotter in this compartment? "Uninvolved."

"Uninvolved. Your same fire team member suggests you were involved with Ysabet, at least sexually. He further suggests her noble sacrifice at the end was to protect you."

Today just might be the day Valderrama got a bullet in the head. At close range, even station-safe ammo can bust a crater in that sick head of his. "She's just a kid, was just a kid. We were never together."

Nassien typed something and then swung the console around to Kay. "She was not who she seemed."

Kay scanned the screen. It had an image of Ysabet, along with medical gibberish she didn't follow.

"Your 'kid' was a genetically-altered Terran infiltrator. Her autopsy gives her an age three years beyond your own. We don't have access to the Net to investigate how or when she got assigned to your squad, but discovering that information will be a top priority when this mission is over."

Kay stared at Ysabet's image. The first live Terran she'd ever spoken to, and she never knew. Did she feel any affinity to her fellow Terran? She couldn't wrap her head around it with Nassien staring at her. "Still looks like a kid to me."

"Indeed." Nassien returned the display to its normal position and leaned back. "That leaves us with a Marine contingent that cannot leave the ship, and a Black March that is not up to the necessary company strength."

"Yes, Ma'am, and two groups with a serious grudge against each other."

Nassien drummed her fingers on her desktop for a moment. "And how would you handle this situation to improve the tactical viability of this mission?"

Kay could have taken the easy way out, saying the mission was dead in the water, but Ysabet as a spy grated on her. She could admit Halabi's involvement, but that would only roast her own skin, and maybe Jax as well. No, if she could help this mission succeed she would, just to screw Halabi and his Terran cohorts, if they really were working together. He'd dragged her into this mess, and she wanted to pay that bastard back any way she could. The answer was obvious.

"Train Marines to replace the lost Black March troops and continue the mission with that full company."

Nassien continued to drum her fingers on the desk. "There's no suitable training facility on this ship, plus, each exoskeleton is built to fit the soldier."

"You must have training simulation programs for a trip this long. And technicians to support hardware that complex. We have six more weeks in space. With ship's personnel and Marine assistance, you could adapt part of the well deck for training and select Marines to supplement your troops based on closest physical match to the remaining exoskeletons. The technicians could make alterations to adjust the fit."

Kay could just glimpse the slow smile spreading on Nassien's face as the finger drumming came to a sudden stop. "So your gene line does have some potential after all."

Kay shrugged. "Halabi wouldn't agree with you."

Nassien stared at her for a moment. "Halabi?"

"My program manager, Ma'am."

Nassien returned to her console, typed a few things in, then stared at whatever she'd pulled up. It kept her attention for long enough that Kay started to fidget to remind Nassien that she was still in the office.

Nassien waved a hand at her. "Your proposal has merit. Flesh it out and send me a full report on how you'd implement it by the end of first shift today. Dismissed."

Nassien never looked up from her console. Kay saluted to the air and marched out. A formal proposal? How did she get roped into that? More importantly, how could she foist off any future tactical credit for the idea onto someone else? Jax, maybe? This was the kind of shit that led to more attention than she wanted. She should have kept her big mouth shut.

Another Marine stood in the passageway, waiting his turn, but Kay didn't give him any reassurance. She wasn't sure what had just happened, other than she'd opened her fat mouth about an idea that she now had to spend the rest of the shift working up. No good deed goes unpunished.

KAY STOOD IN the assembly area on Deck 3 with twenty-two other Marines. No one else knew what was going on or why they were present, but she did, and she cursed herself for ever thinking up this crazy idea. She'd pay for it dearly if the rest found out about her role in this mess.

The group was a jumble of soldiers that crossed squad and platoon boundaries. Taken out of their normal structure meant they had no real order to how they stood in formation. Their individual selection for this "honor" wouldn't make any sense at all unless they happened to be the one who wrote up the plan that specified the requirements. She'd filtered the entire Marine company based first on physical characteristics of height, weight, and body build, to match the existing exoskeletons. Then the psych profiles came in, to filter again based on adaptability criteria. That was the more difficult parameter to measure, but based on depth and breadth of records that the military kept on each soldier, it wasn't hard to write a comparative analysis routine that plucked out the most likely candidates to survive six weeks of intense Black March training.

It also wasn't difficult to realize she and Jax would be present, given their gene line studies. It was just the luck of the draw that two dead Black March soldiers fit their body types. There were two empty exoskeletons to fill, and once they'd passed the physical selection, it was all but guaranteed they'd pass the rest.

"I should have programmed us out of the running for this race," she whispered to Jax, who stood next to her for the start of this idiocy.

"You'd have been caught," he said.

She looked down the line at Valderrama. He turned to her with a confused frown. She gave him a cheery wave that just darkened his glare. That was one little alteration she did to the results that no one had caught. She knew from experience he wasn't at all adaptable, but a few small changes to his results guaranteed him a spot at this circus with the rest of them. It was just a small deposit on the payback she owed him for screwing her over with his riot report and other rumors. Let the bastard stew inside his new Black March suit.

The hatch to the well deck opened, letting in the construction noise resulting from the other part of Kay's big mouth plan that got her standing here with her duffel bag at her feet, like everyone else.

Nassien stepped through the hatch, along with her remaining bodyguard. Marines snapped to attention as she walked along their front line, examining each soldier as she passed. Kay expected as much and hid herself and Jax as far in the back as possible. Still, she felt Nassien's eyes pause on her for what felt like an age before moving on. No one but Jax knew this foolish idea was hers, and she wanted to keep it that way.

Nassien marched back to the center of the line and snapped to attention to face them. The Marines stood just that smarter in response.

"I'll keep it simple," she said. "This mission requires a full company of Black March soldiers. For those of my troop lost or injured from the explosions, you are their replacements."

The assembled Marines grumbled at each other but nobody looked up at Nassien.

"Your commanders have been informed, your transfer orders are in place and will be transmitted to headquarters the instant we leave hyperspace. From this point forward, you are Black March."

The assembled soldiers stared at one another.

"You're idea as well?" Jax whispered.

"Shit no." That wasn't part of Kay's plan. Nassien put her own spin on it. It was only supposed to be a temporary assignment.

The grumbling grew louder around Kay until Nassien paced the front line again to stare down the obvious noisemakers. The now ex-Marines went quiet. Kay was dead meat if they ever found out the seed idea had come from her. No one in their right mind volunteered for Black March. They got the suicide missions. Glory for those that survived, but not a lot of them ever survived.

"We also lost two mission-critical specialists in the explosion. All Black March will be assessed as potential replacements. Your test times and details have been transmitted to you. Meanwhile, exchange your Marine uniform for Black

March black fatigues at the ship's store and pick up your squad and berth assignments. You will be spread out through the experienced squads. At 13:00, you are back here to be fitted into your exoskeletons. Boot camp starts tomorrow at 05:00. Dismissed."

Nassien marched back toward the well deck where they were building the training facility.

"Any idea what's going on back there?" Jax asked once they were alone in the passageway.

"The well deck construction? Some of it. It's our new training site."

The training resource needs was the one part of her plan that she didn't have enough information to flesh out. The capabilities of the Black March exoskeletons were a close-kept secret, one that Nassien wasn't willing to share. Kay could only estimate what some of the extended-range enhancements meant.

"I recommended some details, but Nassien or one of her Black March platoon leads set up the training program." Kay was as in the dark about what Black March boot camp would entail as the rest of the unhappy group.

"What's that testing all about then?" Jax asked as he climbed up a ladder to Deck 2.

"A targeting simulation. There's some special defenses at the site, and they want someone trained to use it if necessary." She glanced back at the closed hatchway to the well deck before climbing the ladder, itching to see what they'd come up with, based on her rough drafts.

Jax nudged her out of her reverie. "You think we're getting fresh uniforms, or the ones they laundered off the corpses before they spaced the bastards?"

Kay turned away from the well deck hatch and scrambled up the ladder. "Does it matter? We're still the walking dead in their exoskeletons." It would matter, though, to some of them. In her rapid strategy session, she didn't consider the psychological effect on those who were filling in for the dead.

As they caught up with their new mates at ship's stores, she could sense that uncomfortable undercurrent around her.

Squads and platoons always had replacements to fill after a battle. After a particularly devastating loss out in the field, platoons could be restructured, but this was different. They weren't just filling in a Marine platoon. They were exchanging their old lives to take on the roles of the dead—the uniforms, racks, and equipment, all in a matter of days. It didn't take a psych genius to know this wasn't going to go well.

Kay stood an hour and a half in line to get her replacement uniforms in two neat packages. At least she got to keep her old boots.

Jax reordered his gear to precise folded perfection. "What's next?"

Kay shoved her new gear in her duffel bag, next to her few personal possessions and her travelling pharmacy. "Now we find our new squad assignments."

Jax expression clouded. "Any chance we're in the same squad?"

Kay shrugged. "No idea." Nobody asked her for opinions on that one.

"They should have sent out assignments by now." He pulled out his data pad. "Great. They posted assignments outside the bunks on the deck we just left."

She shouldered her duffel bag and followed Jax back the way they'd come. She pushed up through the ex-Marines clustered around their new assignment list displayed on the communication board outside the Deck 3 berth hatch. No one looked in a rush to go meet their new squad mates. Who could blame them? Marine and Black March blamed each other for the explosions and the riots. Out here, they were still Marines. Once they stepped through the hatch, they would be a very small group of newbie Black March soldiers. Nassien had her hands full with this mess.

"Looks like you flunked out before we even started." Valderrama laughed at her as she edged closer.

She glared at him. "At least I won't have to deal with your snoring anymore."

Jax squeezed in beside her at the board and scanned the list. "Nassien paired us each up with one of the Black March. I'm with Tajex."

Great. Which clown did she get saddled with? She scanned the board for her gene line designation. What she saw instead was her nickname, Deetchu, K. She had a bunk assignment but no partner or fire team designation. Instead, she had a note to report directly to Nassien. "Shit." How much worse could this gig get?

Jax patted her shoulder. "Good luck."

Kay straightened out her duffel bag on her shoulder and pushed back through the reluctant ex-Marines. She stepped through the hatch, and Jax followed. The Black March berths were significantly different from the ones they left behind. They still had the three stacked racks lined up on both sides of an extra-long compartment. The differences were in the racks themselves. Instead of minimal headroom per rack, they were staggered in the stack so each rack had room enough to sit up at the head of the mattress. They had under-rack storage as well as small lights and privacy shades. Kay found her assigned rack two rows from Jax and dropped her duffel bag beside her bottom rack.

"Nice setup," Jax said over the noise of the other soldiers searching for their new racks.

"One of the perks for being suicide troops," Valderrama said on his way by.

Kay stripped completely and put on her new black uniform. She took out her pharmacy and stuffed enough in her pocket to get her through the day. She stowed the remainder and the rest of her gear in the under-rack storage. She picked up her crumpled Marine uniform and dry-swallowed a little green pill. Taxoril would be just the right level of soporific to get her through the next few hours.

Report to Nassien. What the hell.

CHAPTER 7

Gene Study—KDTU-02128 Replicant Status-3060 AH

Six replicants from Crèche E transferred to military training within separate branches of Nassien Military. Death of Replicant 3 (R3) from biological pathogen in eighth year considered tangential to viability of gene set. Situational awareness tests result in above average score for all replicants. Additional classified gene set testing initiated for Crèche E per order of M. Nassien (XO). Priority 1 reports to be delivered directly to M. Nassien, bypassing Program Manger. Funding approved for fourth stage, based on preliminary target gene set identified from Gen 3 Crèche E. Gen 4 Crèche F initiated for five replicants.

The trek to the head and laundry facilities brought Kay past what remained of the special Black March berths. Cleanup removed most of the evidence of the explosion, but a long, uneven gap separated the regulation racks from the remaining three rows covered in translucent environmental domes. Each surviving dome had a double stack of racks, some with considerable equipment surrounding them. Lucky for her they were empty. She'd rather meet those occupants in their exoskeletons than face to face, if they were that far removed from Novan standard genetics.

She stuffed her brown Marine uniform in the laundry shoot to be picked up by ship's store personnel. It was a shorter trek from there to the now-familiar passageway that led to Nassien's quarters. She paused before the hatch. Why the hell was she here instead of with the rest of the walking dead? In her experience, being singled out never won her any perks. In some instances, it was hazardous to her health. What was Nassien up to? No time like the present to find out. She buzzed on the hatch comm and waited.

One of Nassien's ever-present bodyguards let her in, the same one who'd pinned her to the deck during the riot. Guess the other hadn't recovered yet. The quarters looked the same, except the prayer-room hatch was shut and Nassien was already at her console. Kay inhaled her scent as she saluted. Damn, if it wasn't an extra distraction she didn't need.

"At ease." Nassien spoke again in Terran. What was her obsession with that? Kay should have asked Jax if she used one of the Tarquin languages with him.

"Your proposal has been accepted, obviously. Just as obviously, your squad assignment is irregular."

Irregular spelled trouble, always had, always would.

"First squad reports directly to me as company commander. They are my command squad, handling tactical issues for this mission. Unfortunately, more than half of that squad is dead. Their replacements lack certain skills, skills which you will provide."

Kay glanced to the sole bodyguard but he registered no reaction.

A tight smile curled Nassien's lips. "I believe in efficiency. Chumo who is recovering from injuries incurred during the post-explosion rescue operation, and Malik, with whom you are already acquainted, are my personal guards and part of First Squad. Tajex, who is now First Sergeant for the company, is also in First Squad. The others are of little consequence as they provide no unique skills."

Jax was obviously lumped into that no unique skills category. "What is my role, Ma'am?" Get to the point.

Nassien's smile widened as if she'd just won a card game. "I am in need of a new assistant. You will fill that role."

Kay's eyes shot up to Nassien's and then darted back down. Bad enough to be singled out by the C.O., but to be Nassien's personal assistant as well? Too much trouble happening here, and far too much visibility for her liking.

"You may look at me." Nassien spoke in Novan for Malik's sake, or really for Kay's sake so Malik didn't squash her like a flea for not maintaining that inferior stance.

Kay clenched her jaw and looked directly at Nassien, for the first time long enough to actually see her. Dark, near-black eyes looked back at her from beneath gracefully arched eyebrows and high cheek bones that had to come from the African Nomani genes. Full lips and a narrow chin completed the aristocratic face. Kay's stare lasted long enough to warrant a lifting of one of those eyebrows and a gentle shift to Nassien's pheromones, not enough to register as attraction, but definitely a reaction.

Kay glanced at Malik, but he remained an alert but impassive block. Either he didn't notice the shift, or didn't care. How did he maintain that balance between being present and not present? Must take some practice.

Nassien's chair creaked as she leaned back. "As my assistant, you will discover rather quickly that I remain a target of interest to my opponents. Not all of my enemies are on the other side of this war, either. Your own project manager, for instance, Mr. Halabi. Let us just say there's no love-loss between our families. And that brings us to you, Jax, and Tajex, and where you fit in all of this." She slowly rocked her chair back and forth as she watched for Kay's reaction.

Years of being under the microscope kept Kay from fidgeting, but sweat dripped down her back. Her mind raced for an appropriate response. Admitting that Halabi recruited her to sabotage Nassien's mission seemed like the suicidal response. She opted for something less self-incriminating, but basically honest. "Halabi's out to terminate my gene line, and he's already terminated Jax's line, as evidenced by Tajex's presence in your troop."

"True. We've learned, though, that one of the best ways to guarantee loyalty in the Black March is to be the person to rescue the remnants of a terminated line from physical termination after program termination. The company commander personally selects new recruits into her elite company of fighters."

Death now or death later. Nice strategy, and it likely worked if the commander picked based on the right psych profiles.

"Mr. Halabi has had more success with unofficially terminating your gene line than you know," Nasien continued. "You are the last survivor from your crèche. Since taking over your gene line, he's placed every one of your clone sisters in high-casualty assignments."

Shit. That was more information than she wanted to know about her duplicates. There were other crèches, her own designation of H said there were at least many older ones, and likely one or two younger.

"The question is then, what is Mr. Halabi's plan for you?"

Kay assumed the question was rhetorical. Her shirt clung to her back, making the stiff uniform that much more uncomfortable. She needed to keep a tight lip on what Halabi had said to her if she wanted to keep her skin. Nassien wasn't stupid, but maybe Halabi was. He'd left a strong enough trail behind that Nassien was sniffing around.

"I rescued Tajex from physical termination," Nassien said. "I am sure of his loyalty, and he can keep an eye on Jax. That leaves you, my personal enigma." She studied Kay again, as if looking for some new clue. "It is entirely possible that you are Mr. Halabi's target on this mission, and not me, or at least not me directly. Yours was the only gene line personally selected by my paternal grandmother."

Kay felt her face flush, and she bit her cheek to keep from swearing. Her life of hell started because of this woman's grandmother.

Nassien nodded. "I see that's gotten your attention. Yes, my family is personally responsible for your existence here. I will not apologize for their decisions. But note that Halabi quite possibly hates my grandmother more than he hates me.

Destroying your gene line may just be a way to get back at her. She was instrumental in removing his family from senior status in the Nassien clan."

Kay's drugs were starting to kick in, dampening her anger and loosening her tongue. She couldn't help herself. "You're related to him?"

"Yes, distantly. The Nassien family is sizable. Halabi is from a minor sept, like a distant cousin, but close enough to the power structure at one time to hold a grudge when my grandmother removed his sept and stripped them of the right to use the Nassien name. His destruction of your family points to a grudge beyond me."

"I have no family."

Nassien leaned forward. "Don't be stupid. Your gene line is your family, assuming anything is left of it. Clan is everything."

Nassien's vehemence reflected the common Novan view. Well, Kay had no clan, regardless of what Nassien thought. It was her and Jax. Well, her and Jax before Tajex showed up. Jax could be pretty Novan about his gene line, and she didn't like the idea of becoming a threesome. She'd have to sound him out when she got the chance. If this interrogation ever ended.

"Whatever else he's doing," Nassien said, "Mr. Halabi is definitely out to discredit my grandmother through you." She drummed her fingers on the desk. "I will not let that happen and neither will you. Tajex is my XO by rank and seniority, but I need more tactical support than he is capable of on his own to complete this mission. You will supplement his tactical decisions."

"Ma'am? As your personal assistant?"

Nassien shrugged. "You've only yourself to blame for that. I studied your records, along with the rest of your gene line. If we wanted to isolate the stubborn gene, your family would have been the perfect candidates. Beneath that personality quirk, though, is a definite pattern of exceptional situational awareness topped with a brilliant eye for tactics. Had you embraced your capabilities instead of hiding them under Jax and others before him, you would be of a high enough rank to bring into my command structure."

If she'd embraced her capabilities, she'd be as dead as the other KDTU grunts. Lurking in the shadows kept her alive. How the hell was she going to do that now, right under Nassien's nose?

"Personal assistant is the only other option available to me to keep you in the loop and attending relevant meetings. Your rank is now Lance Corporal and your records and net access have been updated accordingly." Nassien stood up. "I expect prompt attendance and attention to detail as my assistant. Dismissed."

Kay saluted and stepped out the hatch.

"You will not fail me," Nassien said before the hatch closed.

Don't count on it. Nassien wasn't the first to see some kind of golden ticket possibilities in Kay's gene line. All the rest suffered the sting of disappointment, why should Nassien be any different?

Kay headed down the passageway, ignoring the stiff creases in her new black uniform and the drying sweat. Black hair and black gear was too monotone for her taste. She should dye her hair a different color so it clashed better. Maybe something in the blue shade would get under Nassien's skin and bust her dream of a successful mission on the back of Kay's non-existent special skills.

Jax was waiting for her an hour later on Deck 3, in a random clump with the other ex-Marines outside the exoskeleton lab. No one had a rank or a full squad, so no idea on an official formation. Valderrama was off to the side, so she walked up and stood beside Jax.

He fidgeted with his black shirt collar. "Do they starch these things?"

"Biometrics in the collar. They want good skin contact,"

Kay said. "They like to keep an eye on all their troops, all the time." Nassien had given her access to the full info dump on Black March when she assigned her as personal assistant. Kay didn't waste that. She'd spent the past hour looking up her new outfit, from the tagged regulation uniforms to the complex exoskeleton capabilities. It was going to be a nightmare set of training sessions in those shells. "Nassien's techs have a constant readout from every one of us, pulse and heart rate, the works. It's worse when we get in the suits."

Jax looked her up and down. "Where'd you get all that information?"

"I'm Nassien's newest toy. Personal assistant." She left out the promotion and instead wondered if a tech in one of the labs noticed her drop in heart rate now that her little green Taxoril pill had kicked in. At least they couldn't link it to the changes in her brain waves as well, not until she donned her helmet.

"And I thought my assignment was bad," he said.

Kay didn't get to ask how Jax liked his newfound cousin.

Tajex stepped through the hatch from the lab. "Form a line, by rank. You're about to be fitted to your new exoskeletons."

Line formation with no rank insignia meant a lot of chatter and shuffling. Kay took her position right beside Jax. Valderrama swore under his breath, recognizing her new status even before Jax did. Two other Lance Corporals stood next to her, and then the line wrapped to pick up the various Privates, First Class, and Privates.

Tajex gazed across the makeshift line forming in front of him. His eyes paused on Jax but not long enough for anyone else to notice. So he knew the kinship as well.

"The techs will call you in based on your fire team. Cooperate with them as your life depends on their skills to keep your suit tuned to your biomechanical and neurological needs." He stepped back through the hatch.

Kay waited her turn in relative silence, settling into her drug-induced calm. Techs led groups into the suit bays by groups of four, starting with Jax's group. With barely a glimpse of the lab through the open hatch, Kay didn't get to watch Jax fitted into his exoskeleton. About fifteen minutes later, the next group was called in. Those in suits took a different exit out of the lab that led to the assembly area. Kay closed her eyes and hummed while she waited.

"KDTU . . ." A balding tech struggled with her designation.

"That's me." No one else was called up in Kay's group. She didn't stick out enough, now she had to be handled in isolation because her fire team consisted of Nassien and her two bodyguards.

Kay followed the tech through the hatch. The lab was a double-wide compartment lined with exposed exoskeletons held up on cranes. The tech led her down an extra-wide walkway past racks of electronic equipment that filled the space between those suit bays. She eyed up the exoskeleton in the suit bay they stopped at. It was open like a split beetle, with the upper section separated from the lower torso and legs.

The tech turned to her and without actually looking at her, started what was obviously a rote speech. "The outer black shell of your suit is triple-thick armor made from a wurzite nanomaterial that can withstand a sustained lasgun blast. The armor protects the inner servo mechanics that enhance your natural strength and reflexes for superior mobility in the field."

Kay scanned the shell in front of her. The dull black armor overlapped in plates at the obvious joints and positions of rotation. The servo mechanics were hidden as the inside was lined with a full-body biometric suit. Everything about it was supersized, including the massive boots. This thing was going to fit her?

The tech waved her forward. "Store your uniform in the bottom shelf and step into the leggings please."

He must be talking about the lower portion of the suit. Kay stripped to her tank and boxers and stowed them. She faced the suit, picked what she thought was the easiest way, and maneuvered into the pants of the biometric suit. They didn't pull on as easy as a standard body suit. A spiderweb of cables and sensors spread from her covered legs into the exoskeleton. She pushed her feet into the massive boots, an unexpectedly snug fit. The boots came up to just below her knee. They locked in place and a belt automatically strapped around her waist. She pressed the rest of her body against the back of the suit and waited.

"I need to adjust for your biometrics and sensor levels." The tech rolled up one of the scanners and connected it to her suit. She got to study his bald spot as he validated the biometrics, adjusted sensors, and finally sealed the lower portion of her suit. Black armor now covered her from the hips down. It wasn't uncomfortable, but she was glad she and none of the selected Marines were at all claustrophobic. It wouldn't be a good feeling to be sealed in completely by this behemoth.

"Try the basics," the tech said. "Left leg?"

Kay lifted her left leg with more effort than she needed. If her torso weren't still strapped to the suit bay she'd have toppled over. Note to self—servomotors more than capable of lifting the seventy-five kilos of armor encasing each leg.

"Right leg."

She lowered her left leg and lifted the other with less effort and more balance.

"It's like moving in a half-G environment," he said. "Keep to slow, easy movements, at least until you have helmet-control. Your suit's servomotors are working at less than a tenth of their capacity right now."

She'd read the specs. Fully suited and trained, she'll be able to run over sixty kilometers an hour without breaking a sweat. More than she could say right now as she waited for another round of fine tuning on her leg armor.

"Okay, get into the upper torso now." The tech went back to his console.

Kay struggled into the biometric shirt. She got her head and shoulders through, and then pushed her fists through the arms. With her arms linked into the exoskeleton and spread out on either side of her, she had to wait for the tech to pull the shirt fully down over her torso. It was going to suck to have to be dressed like a baby before every mission.

The tech snapped her biometric shirt to the pants. She waited through another round of adjustments before he locked the torso and arm shells shut on her exoskeleton.

"Arms this time, and remember, slow movements."

Kay pulled in her left arm, then her right. Under his direction, she twisted at the waist, as much as the suit locking mechanism allowed for. After a short set of adjustments, he released her from the suit bay. She took a slow step forward and stopped.

"Good. Squat and stand, twist around, get a feel for the movements."

She followed his directions and managed not to break anything. Step one, success.

He picked up a black helmet with full-face shielding. "This is your lifeline. It not only controls the suit, it controls you."

He showed her the inside of the helmet. "This hood is one of the most advanced neural nets, connecting you directly to your suit and helmet. I tuned the suit to match your brain pattern and to provide safety limits based on to your Terran neural and physical capabilities. Never use someone else's helmet."

Nice to be reminded yet again how much lower her physical and mental capabilities were compared to her Novan squad mates. She stood still while he rolled over a stepladder and climbed up with helmet in hand. "With practice, you can do this yourself in the field, but I don't recommend it."

Kay closed her eyes as he pulled the hood over her head and then the helmet and locked it to the exoskeleton collar. She opened her eyes. Natural vision was clear though polarized through the face shield, but hearing was muffled through the helmet. She tapped the sides to let the tech know.

He mumbled something she couldn't hear, then fiddled with his console and spoke into his comlink. His voice crackled over speakers in her helmet. "Patience is a virtue. Your helmet is initializing now—basic audio and environmentals. You should see a running status in the upper right of your HUD. Let me know when it says 'pausing for neuro-sync.'"

Kay watched the data stream. Most of it was gibberish, tech details and bio readouts as suit and helmet ran through diagnostics. She was just a bystander for a minute or two until the "pause" message came up.

"It's on pause now," she said. "Does it always take that long for the suit to come online?"

The tech gave her a dirty look. "You've got a long way to go before you're online. Once the suit is tuned to your stats, it will take five minutes and twenty-two seconds to full operational mode."

"Five-and-a-half minutes? That's a long time to stay blind and not-dead in live fire."

He shrugged. "Five-and-a-half minutes from suit-up to operational. You won't be doing that in live fire unless you're some kind of idiot. Don't reboot your suit during the action and you'll be fine."

Great. She'd have to look up what caused a reboot.

The tech took her through another round of basic mobility tests and then gave her conditional-go status. "Your suit's still on basics and will stay that way until the neuro-synch."

"Right. No superpowers until I'm synced." She stepped away from the suit bay. The dull *clank clank* of her armored boots rang out on the deck. Her hearing was back to normal at least. She joined the rest of the newbies in the open assembly area. Black March behemoths like her moved around the area, stretching and bouncing like idiots. She couldn't recognize anyone in their exoskeletons until a sizable one stumbled over to her.

"About time you joined the party." Jax slapped her back. She didn't register anything but the clang of suit against suit. "Tajex has us jogging laps to get used to the feel of the suit. He says it's part of the neuro-sync process. I think he just enjoys seeing us slam into each other."

Guess that answered her question on what Jax thought of his new cousin. She started walking beside him. She kept a wide space from the bulkheads and other joggers to compensate for her supersized armor. It didn't feel much different than a full bio-suit, but she knew the servos were already enhancing her muscles, compensating for the sheer weight of the suit.

Tajex pulled them all in line after the last Marine was suited up and ran a lap or two. "Black March simulation programs for training are full-emersion exercises. They assume a base-level experience in the suits that none of you have. As such, you will complete an accelerated basic training program before you touch the sims. There are only six simulation suites available on this ship so you will be assigned a series of training slots. These are mandatory. When you aren't in suit or in the sims, you will be studying. Your suit is your life, and in the field, there are no techs to babysit if you have a malfunction. You'll memorize how to repair and tune your own suit, and you will practice that skill on the damaged suits in one of the spare labs.

"Now that everyone is suited up, we're going to run you through a full sync regiment. The sync will tune the suit to your individual biometrics, mental, and physical limitations. If we hit no suit issues, you'll be out of here by 19:00 hours."

Great, three more hours of monkey tests. At least when it was over, she'd have time off in second shift to find some better form of entertainment than laughing at supersized toddlers learning how to walk and run again.

CHAPTER 8

Gene Study—KDTU-02128 Replicant Status-3067 AH

Crèche F proceeding on target with accelerated military training scheduled to begin at year 8. Initial active duty results from Crèche E inconclusive. No replicants survived past first year active duty. Full mission debrief and posthumous evaluation under way for each replicant. Preliminary results suggest gene line instability in extreme offensive operations. Classified gene set testing transferred to Crèche F per executive order from M. Nassien.

Kay woke up the next morning with the mother of all hangovers. That would be the last time she'd accept bootleg whiskey from the Navy girl she was screwing. She had enough in her personal pharmacy to get whatever high she wanted without the miserable aftereffects she was feeling right now. She rolled out of her new rack and pulled on her well-and-truly wrinkled black uniform.

Her datapad buzzed in her uniform pocket before she made it to the head. Maybe that was the noise that woke her up. A quick scan showed a message waiting from Nassien. Wasn't it enough that Nassien made her spend half of second shift updating the training plan to account for the deeper details she had access to now on the suit capabilities? She didn't read it until she finished her business and popped some medicine to dampen the hangover.

"Frigging rotgut." The message was thirty minutes old and ordered her to work on her off shift. So much for any sense of personal time.

Nassien was waiting for her outside the Deck 3 well deck,

along with Tajex and Malik, who remained as silent as ever. Did he know how to talk? Kay was beginning to recognize Nassien's little tap-tap-tap against her leg as either a sign of impatience or downright anger. Either way, not the best indicator for Kay's first full day as her personal assistant. Maybe she should have picked a clean uniform for this?

"Promptness, soldier, is expected of you."

She saluted, and Nassien gave it the barest of nods before leading the way into the well deck. The blast of noise that hit them when Malik opened the hatch didn't help Kay's hangover headache but she wasn't going to get sympathy from her new stiff-backed C.O. She was the last to step through the hatch and shut it. The air inside the well deck was frigid. She wrapped her arms around her chest and stood behind Nassien. Half the remaining Marines must have been recruited to do the grunt work for the Navy's engineering crew. That would add to her popularity if they found out it was her idea. Arc-welding sparks flew from every artificial construct, but the well deck was already transformed into Kay's vision.

"This training site will be ready for your initial full-turn on exercises this afternoon," Nassien said over the din of construction. "Walk Tajex through your training proposal."

So much for keeping her involvement a secret. Tajex looked about as interested in hearing Kay's proposal as she was in giving it. She walked to the first fifty-meter construct that stretched the length of the well deck. "We're landing approximately five kilometers from the target, in a relatively flat area. Those five kilometers are up the side of a rough snow-capped mountain. Since we don't have that kind of distance on ship, we'll increase the well deck to 2-G and run laps over obstacles set up here to simulate the uneven terrain to the defense grid around the gene bank. The main purpose is to learn balance and control of the exoskeleton in uneven footing."

She walked them to the next construction site. "This area is set up to provide an approximation of that defense grid.

We will be under fire during these drills, until we get to the perimeter wall over there."

"The grid won't be an issue when we get there," Tajex said. "Either the site will still be under Novan control, or if the Terrans have it, there's no way they can run the grid without a trained Novan tech."

She kept walking toward the short stretch of wall that represented the edge of the minefield. "And you think a trained Novan tech can't be convinced to run the defense grid when they're facing down the barrel of a lasgun?" She turned back to the wall. "The perimeter wall is designed from local material and cannot be detected from aerial reconnaissance. Its sole purpose is to mark the boundaries to the minefield for Novan personnel. Our next area is the minefield, which, as a passive defense, would remain on if the Terrans took the facility. This section trains us to coordinate physical movements with the enhanced HUD overlay of the mine locations."

She spent the next half hour walking Tajex through the rest of her proposal, answering his questions, and watching the disinterested frown on his face disappear. Nassien was silent for the whole tour. At the end, Nassien dismissed Tajex, but Kay wasn't so lucky. Nassien dragged her and Malik back to her quarters where Malik gave her an ear bud and subvocalizer, tuned to his private channel. Then they were off again, up two levels and half way across the ship before Nassien paused outside the hatch to the tactical simulators.

"This is your first full briefing on the gene bank defense plan," Nassien said in Terran Standard. "Listen to everything. Take whatever notes you need to, in Terran Standard. I'll expect your analysis within twelve hours."

Obviously food and sleep weren't a priority. "Yes, Ma'am."

Nassien opened the hatch. "Mission details are classified. If there is a leak and it points back to you, you will be executed."

Sweet assignment.

Kay followed Nassien and the ever-silent Malik into a compartment dominated by a three-hundred-and-sixty-degree display station that hovered over an oval conference table. Every platoon commander stood at attention around that table, including Tajex, while Nassien walked to the far end and took a seat. Stares tracked Kay's progress as she followed behind Nassien and Malik, but nobody commented out loud. Malik stood against the bulkhead on Nassien's left side as the commanders shuffled into their own seats.

With no better instructions to follow, Kay mimicked Malik's stance on the right side of Nassien. She leaned against the bulkhead.

"Don't slouch," he grumbled over the ear bud.

She straightened up and studied the blank display rather than meet any of the glares aimed at her, especially the one from her former company commander, the only Marine present. She pulled out her datapad for good measure and waited for the briefing to start.

Nassien flicked the display on. Two planets rotated into view, one blue-green and the other a smaller gray planet dominated by massive polar ice caps. "With limited landing capabilities at our disposal now, we will need to focus our mission on the gene bank."

The display zoomed into the southern landmass on the gray planet to show a bleak mountainous landscape. "The facilities are two kilometers underground so surface landmarks are minimal. The entranceways are still protected by the local terrain, which blocks any close approach of tanks or other ground-based transport. The defense grid can fire at a two-kilometer range, and then there is the surrounding mine field. The Black March platoons will land here and here." Two green dots appeared on-screen in what seemed a short distance from the black dot representing the gene bank, but was five kilometers out. "Assuming the facility has not been compromised, we will take up defensive positions within the mine field and within the underground bunker. All soldiers will be provided with an interactive HUD map that displays the location of the mines within the field."

Kay's old company commander leaned back until her chair creaked. "And if the Terrans are already there?"

"We eliminate them," Tajex said, not bothering to look at the Marine commander.

The undercurrent of animosity between Black March and Marine hadn't changed much. Marines don't take kindly to being ship bound after a long transfer. Kay wondered if Nassien was even aware of the hostility directed at her.

Nassien's long fingers flew over the console touch screen. The display shifted to show a series of red dots surrounding the minefields. "If the Terrans arrive before us, our objective is to break through their ranks and reestablish Novan control over the gene bank. The defense grid should be a considerable deterrent to Terran control, but in the event that they take over the facility, they will be left with nothing to protect them but the minefield. No Terran can control the grid."

Must be some special Novan techs in that defense grid. They all took it for granted that they would die in any Terran takeover. Kay listened to the rest of the briefing and the arguments brought forth by different platoon commanders. The battle plan shifted in minor ways, but nothing significant from what Nassien originally presented.

Nassien dismissed the commanders, but kept Kay and Malik behind. Once the compartment cleared, she offered Kay a seat and slipped back into Terran Standard. "Initial thoughts?"

So much for having time to think it through. Kay was glad all she'd taken before this meeting was a headache pill. "Why does everyone assume the defense grid techs can't be forced to use the system against us?"

"They are specially selected and trained. In the event of a takeover, they will not allow themselves to be captured alive. It would disgrace their family honor."

Novan honor, again. Maybe they were right and it wasn't a weakness.

"The defense grid is the reason why everyone will be tested

in the targeting simulator, to replace the two dead mission specialists. In the event the local techs are dead, we need trained personnel to take over."

Kay wanted to ask why she had to go through the tests then, if the grid was beyond Terran capabilities, but she kept her mouth shut. She looked back up at the display, which still showed the contingency plan if the Terrans were already on-planet. "Two primary issues I see. One, you're most vulnerable on landing. We're all crammed into two landing craft. A well-placed ground-to-air missile could take out half your troops. Second, I think you're giving up too easily on the monazite mines."

Nassien folded her arms and leaned back. "Black March landing craft have state-of-the-art armor and are well-armed."

Kay shrugged. "Fine. Twenty well-placed missiles. Either way, the Terrans could get lucky, especially if they have a destroyer in orbit over the planet. Plenty of spare firepower there to take out two landing craft that have no way to hide from ship sensors. If the Terrans are in-system for the gene bank, they know you'll be coming to defend it. And they will know that if they've gone to ground inside the facility, the only way to get them out is with soldiers. You said yourself it's impenetrable to bunker bombs. If it were me, I'd have all my missiles pointing to the sky, waiting for you to show up."

Nassien smiled. It erased all the frown lines and enhanced the natural beauty of her narrow features. Kay looked away. Wrong time for those kinds of thoughts.

"Point made," Nassien said. "Provide alternatives in your full analysis. Meanwhile, what do you propose we do for the monazite mines when we have no way to land or extract Marines?"

"You do. You have two Black March ships."

Nassien lifted one eyebrow. "Won't they be rather busy avoiding your Terran missile attack?"

Kay leaned forward on the table, a plan already half formed in her mind as she visualized the planet. "They won't be landing on that planet at all. Black March suits support high-orbit insertion." She waved her hand across the tabletop. "You scatter us like seeds in a two-kilometer radius around the site instead of five kilometers out where you needed a flat landing space. After Black March insertion, take the transports back here to shuttle Marines to the monazite mines."

Nassien studied her for what felt like ages, tapping the table as she stared. "Put it all in your analysis."

"In Terran?" Kay asked.

"Of course." Nassien stood up, but Kay didn't. "Questions?"

Kay stood. It was dumb to question, but she was fed up with being made to stick out. "Ma'am, why Terran?"

"Why? Because you are the most underutilized resource I've ever come across, Kay." It was the first time Nassien had used her first name or what she pretended was her first name. "You can clearly outthink most of my command staff in one short briefing, but you won't unless I force you to. Maybe if you improve your Terran Standard, you can transfer into something you will apply yourself to, Intel or Terran Tactical analysis. With your looks, you'd make a fantastic spy." She lifted a hand to Kay's hair but stopped short. "Let this grow out its natural blonde and you'd make a beautiful spy."

This time there was no denying the pheromone shift. Kay knew she was incapable of a responding shift, but the blush she felt creep up her cheeks would be just as traitorous a giveaway of her own attraction. This couldn't be happening, not with someone so far up the command chain. She felt a moment's panic before Nassien broke eye contact.

"Your analysis, in Terran." Nassien opened the hatch. "Dismissed."

KAY HAD JOTTED down just enough notes to jog her memory for the analysis she owed Nassien later that night. She had to admit, her plans weren't half bad. She didn't know whether to thank Nassien for pushing her, or hate her for making her more visible and that much more vulnerable if something went wrong. And something, in her experience, always went wrong.

She had to rush to her mandatory targeting sim test, a waste of time if there ever was one.

Kay stepped out of the simulator hatch and ran her fingers through her hair. Something about that sim made her head feel like a hundred spiders were crawling around inside. She had just enough time to eat before another Black March suit session—four grueling hours of training to look forward to before she could finalize her report for Nassien. The training included their first full-suit power to complete the sync up. That called for another little green mellow pill to keep her sane until this long day was over. She dry-swallowed the pill and headed for the mess hall.

KAY STEPPED INSIDE the one mess hall on Deck 3 that they were all still sharing. Navy MPs, the only neutral party, were scattered throughout the hall to keep order. One big, happy military family. She glanced at the Marine section, seeing a few familiar faces from her old platoon, but didn't bother heading that way. They'd made it clear the last time she tried to join them—no black uniforms allowed.

She plopped food on her tray from the line—beans, a mystery vegetable, a synthmeat burger, and juice—and looked around for friendlier faces.

Jax waved her down where he sat with Valderrama and Tajex. Hell, even Valderrama seemed friendly, though she could have done without seeing Tajex again. Lucky for her he left as she approached.

"Where have you been?" Jax shifted to make room for her.

"Took my targeting sim test." She rammed the burger in her mouth to end that conversation track. It was the most grueling targeting simulator she'd ever experienced, with more firing options and tracking detail rammed into her brain than she could handle. The spiders in her head were transforming into the mother of a headache from it.

Valderrama picked up the slack. "We're up a pay grade, did you notice? Guess that's one perk to being cannon fodder now."

"We're less fodder in those suits," Kay said. "It would take a hell of a bullet to penetrate that armor."

Jax picked at Kay's vegetables and helped himself to a clump. "We'll be carrying the right ammo to do it, but let's hope the Terrans won't be, because the suit has weaknesses, according to Tajex. It's full-suit power on today. Any ideas what that means?"

Kay had plenty, but wasn't going to share it. So far, everyone but Jax and Tajex thought she'd just been sidelined as punishment for the riot. That was better than knowing she was Nassien's pet experiment.

"We're about to find out." Valderrama stood up with his empty tray. "Try not to make us look like losers again, Terran."

Kay flipped him off as she rammed the last of her burger down. It was almost comforting to have him be the same old asshole. She spent too much time under Nassien's glare lately, and that entanglement could only get worse over time.

"Come on. Suit-up time takes forever." Jax grabbed her tray and headed out. She followed, wiping her mouth on her sleeve.

AFTER THE SECOND time being helped into her exoskeleton and dragged through a suit check, Kay realized just how much she was going to hate the thirty-minute ordeal. It would be great protection in live action, but, in the meanwhile, she was glad for the mellow drugs she'd popped to dull her mind from the boredom. That it also dulled the insane track her mind was on with Nassien was an added benefit.

She had a different tech this time, an older dark-skinned woman with short, tight, black curls who called her "dear" a few too many times.

Kay was suited up and ready, but still locked into the suit bay.

"Okay, dear. We're going to full biofeedback enabled. Are you ready?"

Kay clenched her jaw. "Yes." Just get it over with.

The tech fiddled on her console, and Kay's vision blurred as a tingling sensation ran through her, starting at her scalp and eventually extending right to the tips of her gloved fingertips. It wasn't exactly unpleasant, just disorienting.

"How's that feel, dear?"

"A little dizzy."

The tech let out a sigh of relief. "That's good. There's more to the brain than we can map, so there's always a risk at first turn-on. Not to worry though, I haven't lost anyone yet."

Was that meant to be comforting? Kay squeezed her eyes shut and then opened them. No change. The tech went back to her console and fiddled.

Kay's vision cleared. She felt better. Much better. "That's great."

"Good. The suit learns from you over time so it will adapt to your capabilities." She patted Kay's armored shoulder and to Kay's surprise, she could actually feel it. That could get downright freaky in some circumstances.

"They'll take you through full turn-on next. Take it easy out there, dear."

The assembly area filled up with oversized black bulks flexing their new suits. Kay recognized Jax and lined up next to him. "More techs?" She pointed to the bulkhead.

"They get to flip our switches." He looked as uncomfortable in his suit as she felt.

"It's only the full turn-on test. Once we pass this, nobody flips our on switch again but us." At least she hoped that was true. She didn't like giving anyone control over her, and in this suit, that control was a whole lot more than figurative.

Tajex paced in front of them in his own exoskeleton. "Your suit adapts to you, but that takes more hours than we have left to train on this mission. We've set up an accelerated training and adaptation program to get you through that will get you maybe eighty percent of the way to full integration. It's the best you can hope for."

"Inspirational," Kay whispered.

Jax grunted in reply.

"The techs will enable full turn-on in groups of five. Once enabled, you'll run three laps, and then stand down for the next group. You will definitely feel the difference from what you've been feeling in your suits prior to turn-on."

Kay waited her turn with Jax. It was obvious when full turn-on occurred. Each soldier jolted as if hit with an electric shock. One at a time, they took off in what turned into a race around the assembly area, only they weren't used to their suits yet. Jax swore when the first one misjudged a turn and slammed into the bulkhead at what must have been close to forty kilometers per hour. The soldier was up and running again in less than two seconds. After that it was more comedy than worry as soldiers collided, bounced, and otherwise whipped around in a frenzy of miscalculated moves.

"We're next." Kay stood stiff, waiting for the turn-on and the chance to join the fun.

It hit her like it hit everyone else, with a physical jolt. Her sensory perception was enhanced beyond anything she'd imagined. Visually, she saw a spectrum beyond even Novan eyesight, heat-enabled, and distance automatically tracked. She could focus on sounds or isolate background noise. Even her olfactory sensation was enhanced. That was the first control she dampened. Ex-Marines stank enough without hyper senses.

Jax was grinning like a kid on a candy high. "Try not to let me lap you."

He took off in a burst of speed around the arena, and Kay was on his tail in an instant. Exhilarating didn't adequately describe the feeling as she took the first corner in a skid. Part of her brain knew the neural net enhancing every part of her—physically and mentally—induced the euphoria but she wondered how much the drugs in her system were altering the experience. If this feeling all came from the suit, she'd save a mint on her personal pharmacy purchases. She slammed into the bulkhead on her first real miscalculation but used her momentum to bounce off and leap in front of Jax in the race.

"That's cheating!"

"All's fair in love and war, my friend." She ricocheted off the bulkhead once again to bounce in front of another soldier but misjudged this time and landed in a clump on the deck. The suit took the impact, and she sat more dazed by her error than the physical hit. Jax sped past her with a wave.

"Smug bastard." She shot up after him for their last lap. She wasn't going to beat him so she made the only logical choice. With one super-powered leap, she flew through the air and body slammed him into the deck.

He rolled her off with a laugh. "You never could take second place, could you?"

The other three soldiers finished in front of them as they jostled their way to end their final lap.

Kay wasn't even winded by the run. "Hell of a nice suit, eh?"

Jax bounced on his toes, an effort that shot him up a meter in the air each time. "That it is, that it is."

The natural high from having superpowers in the suit didn't last the full training session. Even with enhanced capabilities, it was a grueling training program. Powered down and out of the suit, Kay was exhausted. Coordination didn't come magically after sync-up, so she wasted a lot of energy fighting the suit rather than working with it, and she wasn't alone. Drained faces appeared out of their helmets all around her as they left the lab.

"I can smell him, you know, when I'm in there," Valderrama said. "The dead guy who used to have my suit."

"They've been fully sanitized," Jax said.

"It's not enough," Valderrama said.

He was right, it wasn't. Kay didn't have Novan senses, but she still felt she walked in a dead man's shoes, and so did the rest of them.

KAY SPENT THE next three weeks bouncing between training and Nassien's staff meetings. She learned who were the bright ones were who were the useless morons. It was obvious that Nassien knew as well, but Kay didn't think the officers picked up on that subtlety.

Three long weeks of grueling training also gave Kay more confidence in the suit. The worst part though, was the superstitious edge that settled on them after the initial excitement of the exoskeleton training. They were wearing the dead soldiers' suits, and there was no easy way to lift that cloud of doom. Jax seemed affected by it as well. His moods were dark, and he didn't bother much with idle chatter, except with her and his new best friend, Tajex. Even she turned to her personal pharmacy to get her through most suit-up sessions, just enough to take the edge off and forget about lingering ghosts.

Tajex stood in front of them in the well deck, where the advanced training courses were finally complete. "Fourth-week training is the last session with just you lot. After this, you'll train in squads and fire teams based on your assignments during the mission."

They were again facing a lineup of technicians, all holding portable suit controllers.

"What's with the techs?" Valderrama asked.

Jax hadn't gotten over the toe-bouncing trick and turned to her for an answer.

Kay had given up on hiding how directly involved she was in their training program. Everyone knew she was Nassien's assistant, and the rest became obvious over time. "They are initiating an overlay program to simulate the mine field. It's like a built-in simulator, through our helmet and HUD."

"So this is where we hopscotch around the mines," Jax said.

Kay watched his rhythmic rise and fall. "Maybe less hop or you'll knock someone into a mine."

"A simulated mine," he said between bounces. At least he was less moody for now.

Kay's mind had already settled into a quiet lull from the double dose of Taxoril. It would be a slow stroll through the simulated minefield for her. A hammer blow to the head wouldn't get past her mellow state.

Tajex called them to attention. "The techs are going to load you up with a simulation program in a minute. You'll feel a little disorientation but it'll go away, and you will see a visual of the minefield. Look for the pattern in the mines to find a safe path through." He signaled to the techs. Each tech fiddled with their controls.

Kay waited to feel the change. She watched as Jax and the others shook their heads for a moment, but she didn't feel anything different. She was about to ask what he saw, when her vision swam. She must have a slow tech controlling her. Her HUD sparkled in a kaleidoscope of colors. She had just enough time to register the change.

Icy pain stabbed through her head and sent needles of pain throughout her body. Her last moment of consciousness was hearing the enhanced sound of her own scream.

CHAPTER 9

Gene Study—KDTU-02128 Replicant Status-3068 AH

Crèche E active duty results from first year show evidence to prove initial hypothesis of exceptional tactical abilities in gene line. Situational awareness tests scheduled to ramp up in 3068 AH for Crèche F. Survival rate over 43% is necessary to move project to first-level Experimental status, but gene line still showing instability for long-term survival in active duty conditions based on Crèche E results. Crèche F military training initiated targeting pilot training.

Kay woke up to the scent of antiseptics. She opened her eyes to an unfamiliar dark ledge above her. It took her a moment to recognize that she was in a lower bunk in sickbay with an IV in her wrist and a monitor beeping beside her. She'd been here enough times recently, but she couldn't remember what put her here this time. She took in her surroundings in a slow moving turn of her head. A tray with ice water sat near her head. The bunks next to her were empty, but the set against the far bulkhead were covered in a stasis dome, victims from the explosions who were too far gone for the ship facilities to care for.

Her mouth was dry, and her head throbbed with a dullness that came from painkillers. She shut her eyes. What had she been doing? Suit training. The memory of that blinding pain came back to her. What the hell did she do wrong?

Raised voices nearby, one in particular, convinced her to open her eyes again. The empty bunk above her shaded out the overhead lights, which was good since the little light that came through hurt her eyes. Nassien was at the foot of her bunk, her hand tapping out an angry tattoo against her thigh again. Someone was in trouble. What had she done wrong? Did she ruin the suit somehow?

She shifted her head to catch a glimpse of whomever Nassien was arguing with, but the movement hit her head like a sledgehammer. She closed her eyes and bit down on an embarrassing moan.

Not well enough though, as Nassien was at her side when she opened her eyes again. Kay looked into those brown eyes and felt more naked in her hospital gown than if she really were naked. She tugged up the edges of the hospital blanket to give herself something to do besides blush.

"Are you in a lot of pain?" Nassien asked in Terran.

Kay tried to speak but all that came out was a dry rasp. Nassien picked up the ice water cup with a straw and held it to Kay's lips. She swallowed with some difficulty. The attention made her even more uncomfortable. She drank only enough to help her speak. "Only hurts when I move, Ma'am."

"That's to be expected." Nassien hooked a stool closer with her boot and sat down.

It was even more disconcerting to see her at almost eye level in Kay's current condition. Whomever Nassien argued with had disappeared, leaving Kay with just her, her bodyguard, and a couple of human ice cubes who would ride out the mission in stasis until they could get the complex medical attention they needed.

"It could have been worse. Those drugs in your system blocked a good part of the hit."

Blocked? She couldn't imagine what it would have felt like if she'd gotten the full force of that meltdown. What kind of trouble was she in, now that she'd screwed up her suit and was caught high on drugs? She ignored that half of her problems for now and focused on the suit. "What went wrong?"

Nassien's lips thinned to a tight line. "Someone sabotaged your suit. Instead of receiving an overlay simulation, you got a suit recalibration, nominally to Novan standards."

Just what she wanted, another reminder of just how far below Novan standards she was, enough to knock her unconscious. "Was it just my suit that got hit?"

"Yes. I have my own technician investigating the program. She thinks it was meant to look like the Novan program was an accident, but the effects on you prove otherwise. A standard Novan brain profile could have caused some problems for you after prolonged exposure. Your acute reaction points to deliberate sabotage with deadly intent. We arrested the tech responsible for the attack, but he took a suicide pill before we could interrogate him."

Interrogate? More like torture. The military used whatever means necessary to extract information. Kay was surprised they would go to such lengths on her behalf. Then again, this ship had a history of nefarious events, hers just adding to the pile. Why would one of techs think attacking her was worth dying for? She tried to shake her head, but it walloped her with more pain.

"Stay still." Nassien rested her hand on Kay's arm. The warmth from that contact made it even harder to think.

"I don't get it. Why would someone kill themselves to get at me?"

"You're on my staff, that could be enough."

Or it could be that damned gene line designation, or that she was Terran. Or maybe she'd finally pissed off someone important. Either way, it was deeper shit than she wanted to be in.

"Kay, I'm . . ." Another argument beyond the bunks stopped Nassien short, and she stood up.

Kay took the opportunity to hide more of herself under the blanket.

She saw a familiar red bulk trying to push his way past Nassien's bodyguard. He was trailed by a pair of Navy MPs. "It's Jax."

Nassien took a step back from the bunk and switched back to Novan. "Let him in."

Jax stepped past the guards and paused, his eyes widening as he recognized Nassien, and saluted.

"At ease," she said.

"Sorry to interrupt, ser." Jax twitched like a nervous rabbit. Kay would have laughed if she didn't think the pain it caused would ruin the humor. "Just came to check on her status."

Nassien narrowed her eyes and glanced from Jax to Kay. "You have been in the same squad with him for years. Do you trust him?"

Kay nodded. Shit! She had to stop doing that. She managed not to embarrass herself with a moan again as the pain shot around her head like it was an empty case.

Nassien took a step closer, then frowned and turned back to Jax. "You will stay here and guard her until I can make other arrangements."

Jax stiffened. "Yes, ser."

Nassien left, taking her bodyguard but leaving behind the two Navy MPs.

Jax relaxed after she left and folded himself down to sit on Nassien's stool. "What was that all about?"

Kay wished she knew. Something was rattling Nassien, and she wasn't ready to admit it might be her. "She thinks someone is out to get me. Some tech tried to fry my brain in that suit."

He curled his hands into big red fists. "Who did it?"

"Doesn't matter, he's dead already."

"Good." He looked around at the I.V. plugged into her arm. "How bad is it?"

"Not too bad. Free drugs." Speaking of which, she'd been caught with illegal drugs in her system. That was going to come back to haunt her sooner or later.

"I don't like it," he whispered, looking around. "You're too close to Nassien now."

Kay couldn't stop the blush but Jax didn't seem to notice as he continued his diatribe.

"Why did she have to pick you, anyway? She could have grabbed anyone else to fill in her staff."

"Nice to know my best friend thinks any other grunt can fill my shoes."

"You know what I mean. She singled you out, and who knows why." He looked back at her. "Maybe this was a good thing."

"Getting my brain fried?"

"She'll have to get someone else to replace you now as her assistant."

Kay hadn't thought of that. Would she want off Nassien's staff? Hell, would it even matter, if she were the actual target? Trouble would follow her so long as she was trapped on this ship. "I don't think I'll be down for that long anyway."

He leaned forward with an intensity she didn't expect from him. "Milk it then. If you're flat out for a week, you'll be too far behind on the training anyway. You'd be safe on-ship."

Kay glowered at him. "I don't take free rides. When have we ever sat out a mission?"

Jax crossed his arms. "Maybe this is the one you should."

She looked away. "Not going to happen."

He sighed. "You sure they aren't investing in some super stubborn gene with you?"

Kay laughed. "I've heard that's a possibility."

Jax sat with her for hours, missing his own mealtime. Kay slept for some of it. She was just waking up when Nassien returned and dismissed Jax.

"Think about what I said," he whispered. "Stay here as long as you can." He left, with a wary eye on Nassien and the MPs.

Kay could move some without extreme pain, but the persistent headache was grating on her nerves. She just wanted to stay asleep, but that wasn't going to be possible without stronger meds.

Nassien stood at the other side of sickbay, stiff and formal as she pulled her obsidian blade out of its black leather sheath. Both Navy MPs dropped to their knees. Kay leaned forward but couldn't hear what Nassien was saying. Whatever it was, it held the full attention of the MPs and the med tech that stepped into the middle of the ritual and froze. It all lasted only a few minutes, ending with each MP kissing the hilt of her blade before rising.

The look of awe in their eyes was unmistakable, even from a distance, and Kay realized what she'd witnessed. It was the Knife Oath. She'd heard about how the oath had existed on Old Earth and traveled to the stars with the earliest Novan refugees. The highest castes kept it as one of their sacred rituals. Nassien just swore the two Navy MPs to her personal service.

One MP took position at the end of Kay's bunk and the other disappeared. Nassien squatted down next to Kay, eye to eye once again. "It's the best I can do for now. Malik did as complete a background check as he could on these two with ship resources, and I interviewed them myself. One of them will remain with you at all times."

Bodyguards? "Don't you think that's overkill, Ma'am?"

"No, I don't. Your background proves you could be in this mess all on your own, but I can't take that chance. Enough people have died for me already. You will not be the next one."

Guilt was a powerful motivator, and she felt its pull as well, in the face of everything Nassien was doing for her. Her mouth opened before her brain could stop it. "Halabi told me about you before the mission"

Nassien stared at her. "Explain."

Stupid, stupid, stupid. No way to backtrack now. "Nothing specific, Ma'am. Nothing you could hang him for. He just insinuated he'd be happy if this mission didn't turn out well, since it would reflect badly on you."

"On me or my family?"

"He wasn't that specific." Nassien's steady glare unnerved her. That and her condition made it hard to focus. How much was too much to reveal? How much would Nassien figure out on her own now that she'd opened her big mouth?

Nassien shut her eyes and took a deep breath. When she opened them, her gaze was less intense. "You should not be in the middle of this, but I need your help to understand the undercurrents here. I need your loyalty."

The drugs or the deep brown eyes, or her own crazy emotions, Kay gave up. "He said your family owns my contract. He wasn't going to lose any sleep if I proved out his theory that my gene line was a mistake."

Nassien sank down on her knees. "And will you? Prove him out?"

"If I haven't already, you mean."

A quick smile lifted Nassien's lips. "You are not that critical to this mission, not yet anyway."

Her datapad buzzed. She scanned the message and flicked it off. "Don't take credit for someone else's calculated attacks. Whether this is all related to Mr. Halabi's issues with me or not, there is a risk to the mission and more specifically to you."

"And you, Ma'am."

She rested her hand on Kay's shoulder. "You are one of my best tactical advisors. Mr. Halabi cannot change that unless you let him." She stood up. "The MPs will guard you while you recover. Report directly to me when you're released." She left with Malik.

Kay closed her eyes. It was a dumb risk to take, confessing everything to Nassien. She could have ended up back with the remnants of the Marines, or worse, in the brig.

She didn't regret her honesty, whether it was drug-induced or not.

KAY LEFT SICKBAY after thirty-six hours. She had a pocket full of legal painkillers to add to her personal pharmacy. What she wanted to do was grab a meal and crash on her rack. Her second wish was to hunt down Jax and find out what she missed in the training session since she'd had no schedule update on her datapad the whole time she was in sickbay. With her pet MP at her shoulder, she decided neither was worth the effort to explain to her new shadow. How did Nassien cope with it? She walked to Nassien's quarters instead, reporting in as expected. Her pet MP waited by the hatch when Malik let her in.

Nassien stood up as she entered. "You look better." She stepped around her desk and paused in front of Kay. After a glance at Malik, she leaned back against the desk. "I have had your suit moved to a secure area accessible only to me and my personal technician. She is already responsible for my suit and my personal guards. She will take ownership of yours as well. There will not be a re-occurrence of this latest incident."

Incident. Nice euphemism for attempted brain-fry.

"She's already recalibrated your helmet. Do you have any questions?"

"Yes, Ma'am. I'm behind on training, but I have no updated schedule in my datapad."

"Training is by squad and fire team now. As my personal assistant, you control my schedule. You need to work through my appointments to schedule times that we can train together, as a unit. Malik will give you the details. As you say, we are behind so training sessions take priority over all but critical mission briefings."

"Yes, Ma'am." Somehow Kay hadn't considered that she'd be training directly with Nassien. That was an added burden she could have done without right now. Her head was beginning to throb, and she was a good two hours before she could take another pain pill. She did have her own stash, as soon as she got out of this place.

"Also, you'll bunk here now, so the MPs can at least partially resume their normal duties."

Shit. This was way too close. She had a hard enough time fighting against the pheromones during their scheduled meetings. Between training and bunk-buddies, she'd never catch a break. She looked up but Nassien was avoiding eye contact.

"Take Chumo's rack until he recovers." Nassien switched to Novan. "Malik, show Kay to her rack."

"Yes, ser." Malik pushed open the hatch to the left of Nassien's desk and ushered Kay inside.

Was Nassien being over protective, or did she want a close eye on one of Halabi's potential agents? Either way Kay wasn't going to have much freedom left at this rate, between her assignment and suit training. At least she'd get to see Jax during their suit-on training.

Kay pushed aside thoughts of the ridiculous family feud she found herself in the middle of and looked at her new rack. Two racks took up the left-hand side, with storage underneath the bottom. It wasn't as good as the Black March rack she was leaving behind. With her and Malik in the aisle, there was barely enough room to move in the tiny compartment. Cozy.

"Which one is mine?" And where would she go when Chumo came back to active duty.

Malik clenched his jaw, obviously as unhappy as she was to be bunkmates. "Chumo is the bottom rack. His gear is still in the right-hand storage. Yours is on the rack. Minus the drug satchel." He squeezed past her and stepped back through the hatch.

Asshole. He'd searched her gear and dumped the only stuff worth keeping. Now she got to sleep with the rest of her gear. Lucky for her she packed light, with just a spare uniform, extra tank tops, socks, and shorts. With the exoskeleton as her mission suit, she didn't even have a bio suit to keep track of. The loss of her pharmacy was the real stinker. She wondered if that was under Nassien's orders too or if he'd taken that initiative on his own. Since he was Nassien's personal security, he probably did it on his own. He was a clueless git if he thought she couldn't restock the important drugs after a little negotiating with Navy personnel. She'd have to milk her pain meds until she got that chance.

She glanced at her watch. Two hours until her next meal. Like hell she was going to spend it here. Her options were studying suit mechanics or flaking. She stepped back into the main office. Nassien and company were gone. She took a look around Nassien's quarters, but there wasn't much to see beyond the desk and the hatches that led to the bodyguard racks, and that prayer compartment she'd seen earlier that probably held Nassien's rack. With no one to stop her, she opened the third hatch out of curiosity. It was the head. Well, at least she wouldn't have to stumble down the passageway in the middle of the night.

For the main compartment, nothing adorned the bulkhead or desktop, no pictures of loved ones, no trinkets, nothing. It was the kind of quarters Kay would have kept, but felt out of place for a woman who claimed such tight family ties. Then again, Nassien's family ties were out to screw them both over, so maybe it did make sense.

She tapped the console touch screen, but it wasn't coming to life for her. Trust didn't extend that far. She stepped out the front hatch, and it slammed shut behind her. Her own guard dog snapped to attention but she ignored him. Would the hatch open back up for her or would she have to sit in the passageway and wait? She palmed the key entry and heard the clang of the hatch lock open. Trust went that far at least.

She walked down the passageway with her MP in tow.

JAX DROPPED HIS sandwich on his plate. "You're living with her now?"

Kay swallowed a bite. "I'm not living with her. I'm bunking with the frigging bodyguard."

Her MP body stood at attention behind her, constantly scanning the crowd. The guy took his new role too seriously. She couldn't ignore him and neither could Jax, or anyone else who walked by. Always fun to stick out in a crowd. She rammed another fork full of food in her mouth and wondered what it would take to convince Nassien to nix the watchdog.

Valderrama dropped his tray next to her and sat down. He stared at the Navy MP. "What's with the shadow MP? Did they finally arrest your Terran ass after you fried your suit?"

"I didn't fry the suit, someone did it for me. I'd be a hell of a lot safer spending this mission in the brig."

Valderrama let out a harsh laugh. "I knew you wouldn't survive to land-fall. Question is, what makes you so special that Nassien wants to keep you alive. Are you screwing her, too?"

"Trust me, that's not the kind of attention I want."

He didn't reply, which was proof enough that he believed her. No one could spend two years as her squad mate and not pick up how much she avoided attention. The squint in his eye said he still didn't trust her though, but she didn't care. He'd done all the damage he could with the Ysabet accusation, but that got no traction beyond the riot. Was it only four weeks since the kid's death? Or the Terran spy's death. Too much had gone on since then. It was all a freaking mess.

"You haven't escaped either, Jax. Your training is going to be shifted to accommodate Nassien's schedule as well." She stuffed a fork full of pasta in her mouth. "Us, Tajex, and Nassien's bodyguard goons. One big happy squad."

Jax resumed eating but the frown never left his face. "When do we start this new schedule?"

"As soon as I figure it all out, tomorrow I guess." She still had to dig into Nassien's appointment calendar.

After eating, Kay went starboard with her MP to the public access comm room. She sat in front of an open terminal and logged into the ship's mainframe from her official account. She had access to Nassien's calendar as well as the rest of their squad. She opened Nassien's first, anticipating that it would be the busiest, and she was right. A series of color-coded blocks filled up the screen. This wasn't going to be easy.

She scanned the calendar entries. Most she recognized as the regular meetings Nassien dragged her to as her assistant, but there were five short appointments every day, marked personal. Whatever they were, they would make it nearly impossible to find a four-hour block for training on some days. Maybe she could get Nassien to cancel some of them.

She finished what she could an hour later and stepped out of the comm room. The other MP waited for her and tailed her back to Nassien's quarters. "I'm in for the night."

The MP saluted and left as she stepped through the hatch. No one else was around. It was early to call it quits for the day, but where could she go with her MP shadow in tow? The stares got under her skin. Thanks to the shadow, she couldn't hook up for sex, or poke around to restock her pharmacy. She definitely needed to get Nassien to back off on the guards.

She opened the hatch to their berth. Empty as well. She pulled her vid player out of her duffle bag and kicked the rest of her gear to the base of the rack. Somewhere after the second movie she fell asleep.

She woke up hours later. Malik was a snorer. Great. She peeled off her uniform and felt the urgent need to visit the head. Malik's snoring stopped the instant she opened the hatch.

"I need to pee," she said as she stepped out in her tank top and boxers.

The head was a few steps away but she slammed her toe on Nassien's desk in the dark and let out a low curse. Next time she'd bring a light. She took care of business and stepped back out to better lighting. Nassien leaned on the bulkhead outside her hatch in a bathrobe.

"Sorry, Ma'am." Kay saluted.

Nassien stood up. "You didn't wake me. It is almost time for Fajr."

Kay didn't recognize the Novan word, but she did recognize the appraising stare. She hadn't thought about running into Nassien in her underwear. Nassien's gaze paused on her left arm, and she scratched it self-consciously.

"How did you get the scars?" Nassien asked.

"Shrapnel, two missions ago." The one where Yang died, and then they got Ysabet.

Nassien lifted the bottom of her bathrobe to show a brown, well-shaped calf marred by a thin light line. "Laser pistol. One of the first assassination attempts. Before I had Malik and Chumo."

"How old were you?"

"Sixteen." Nassien let the robe fall back down. "Now I need to clean up."

"Oh, sorry." Kay sidestepped to her hatch.

"You apologize a lot."

That's something she'd never been accused of before. She closed her hatch and crawled back into her rack. Sleep wasn't coming back any time soon, not the way her heart was racing.

"Nice mess you got yourself into now," she whispered to herself.

"Hmm," Malik grumbled. She had to agree with that sentiment.

CHAPTER 10

Gene Study—KDTU-02128 Replicant Status-3069 AH

Crèche F development through under-age cycle on track. With the early termination of crèche D and the poor survival rate from crèche E, Program Manager recommendation accepted to halt further replicant crèches until Crèche F maturity level reached at age 15 and active duty results can be analyzed. The future of this gene line under review based on poor active duty results. Project redirection based on Program Manager recommendations approved. Crèche F removed from early pilot training and under review with possible Marine and Army assignments.

After a full shift stuck in Nassien's quarters, Kay realized what those five schedule blocks per day were—Muslim prayer times. Nassien refused to shift any of them to accommodate their squad training, but she did move meetings around so they could have a four-hour squad-based session most days.

On their first training session, Nassien led Kay to a different tech lab on Deck 3. "This is where you suit up now. It should be keyed for your access by now. Try it."

Kay stepped forward and pressed her palm against the hatch key. It clicked, and she turned the hatch handle and stepped inside. Malik and Nassien followed. The compartment was set up as the other tech labs, but much smaller, containing only the three Black March suits for her, Malik, and Chumo, and one slimmer gray suit for Nassien.

The older woman that had been Kay's tech for full turn-on stepped around a lab bench and pulled Nassien into a hug, then held her at arm's length. "Ayaan, you've lost weight, again."

She gave Malik a dark glare. "Can't you make sure she eats better than this?"

Malik kept his face blank, obviously used to this unorthodox technician.

She let go of Nassien and stepped around Malik to study Kay. "And this is your Terran friend. We met before I think, eh?"

Kay cast a quick glance at Nassien, who seemed not at all put out by her technician's familiarity.

"Kay, this is First Technician Nomani."

Of course, the resemblance was there if she looked for it. The technician's skin tone was deeper brown than Nassien's, but they shared the same arched eyebrows and full lips. It was disconcerting to see Nassien's attractive features on the tech's pudgy relative. It made sense, though, who better to trust with the sensitive support of a life-sustaining exoskeleton than a trusted family member.

"First Technician? You Nassiens are obsessed with titles." She extended her hand. "I'm her aunt, from the sane side of the family. Call me Huda. The rank is purely ceremonial to keep Ayaan's mother happy." Huda clasped Kay's hand. "Nasty business with that helmet override, dear. Won't happen again, though. I've turned that capability off in your suit, same as Ayaan's."

Huda got the three of them fitted into their suits. It took longer with just one technician, but she could see why Nassien wouldn't put this task in anyone else's hands, not after that helmet override.

Tajex, Jax, and the two other members of their squad of eight waited for them in the assembly area.

Tajex saluted. "If you are ready, ser, we will start with ground maneuvers."

Nassien nodded assent, and the training began in earnest. Malik paired with Nassien, leaving Kay to pretend she had a partner in Chumo. Similarly, Tajex and Jax were a pair, and the other two the final pair. In twos, they made their way across the obstacles that represented the rocky, mountain terrain. Kay was the laggard in the group, though it felt good to be back in action.

After they'd completed a week together, the biggest thing Kay had learned was the weaknesses in Nassien's suit. That lighter gray exoskeleton shared many of the enhancements her own suit had, including the built-in oxygen supply and pressurization, but physical strength improvements and armor thickness took a back seat to aesthetics. It seemed a risky compromise given that Nassien planned on leading the ground assault. Then again, she'd have two personal bodyguards watching after her, so maybe it wasn't that big a risk.

NASSIEN PULLED KAY out of the mess hall, dismissing her MP shadow. "The Navy XO has called a security meeting, no agenda given."

They marched down the passageway and up two levels to Deck 1. Kay looked around at the Navy officer compartments as she passed, but they were the same drab gray as everything else on-ship. They stepped into a briefing compartment already occupied by the XO, the Marine company commander, and three other Navy personnel. The XO stood at attention as they entered.

"At ease, Mr. Moki." Nassien, as the ranking officer, took the empty seat at the head of the table. Malik stood to her left, leaving Kay to stand at her right. She wondered where she would stand when Chumo recovered. Moki glared at her as if he wanted to object to her presence, but one look at Nassien seemed to convince him otherwise.

He sat down, followed by the rest of the officers. "With your permission, ser?"

Nassien nodded. "Proceed."

He glanced toward a nervous-looking young woman on his right. "My security officer, Specialist Chan, has been studying the incidents relating to your combined company. Miss Chan, if you could bring us all up to date on your findings?"

Chicken shit, Kay thought, not willing to face Nassien himself, he was dumping the responsibility on his junior officer.

Chan cleared her throat a good three times before she began. "We've analyzed the data from the bombings, the riot, and," she glanced at Kay and looked away, clearing her throat again, "and other events, cross-correlating the information and running it through a series of scenario-analysis programs."

Nassien leaned back in her chair. "The results, Miss Chan?"

Chan glanced at her XO, but he wasn't going to give her any help. "The results suggest, ser, that Private First Class designate," she glanced down at her datapad, "KDTU02128-Gen4-H is a major catalyst in these events."

Kay didn't need to mask her surprise because she wasn't surprised at all. Her only thought was whether it was a deliberate setup or if her luck really did suck that badly.

Nassien couldn't have been surprised either, but she leaned forward. "Is that the extent of your analysis?"

Chan swallowed whatever her next words were going to be. Finally, her useless XO stepped in. "We cannot prove your . . . assistant is responsible for these events, but she has been involved in each of them. Given this information and that she is Terran in origin, her continued presence on this mission poses an unacceptable security risk."

Nassien quirked an eyebrow. "Unacceptable?"

The XO blanched. "Well, significant."

"And what do you propose, Mr. Moki."

"She should be confined, ser, for the remainder of the mission. Preferably in the brig."

Nassien's fingers tapped her leg under the table, not a good sign. "I'm sure I needn't remind you that military regulations do not allow for unwarranted incarcerations."

"Ser." The XO glared at Kay. "The individual is Terran, not Novan. The other known instigator was Terran as well. This soldier's legal rights in this instance are unclear."

"Then let me make it clear to you." Nassien's finger tapping came to an abrupt stop. "My assistant has a clean record of performance of duty in the Nassien Military and obviously, as a member of my staff, I have full confidence in her loyalty. Or do you plan to invoke ship's privilege to override my authority?" she added in a much softer tone.

"No, no, of course not." The XO looked like someone just aimed a laser cannon at his head. Then again, that might just be what he faced if he went up against a high-ranking Nassien.

Nassien stood up. "This meeting is over."

"Ser." The XO jumped out of his seat. Malik stepped in front of Nassien, and the XO dropped back down in his chair. "Please, ser. Consider the risk."

"Your concern is duly noted, Mr. Moki." Nassien signaled Kay forward. She opened the hatch and preceded Nassien into the passageway.

Malik followed, keeping watch on the XO. It was the first time she'd seen him come alive, and she was glad his glare was not directed at her. She followed Nassien, keeping her face as blank as possible, but knowing she just made another handful of enemies. She was collecting them faster than ever on this mission.

Her initial calm reaction to the accusations dissolved as they proceeded across the ship and by the time they reached Nassien's quarters, she was pissed at the Navy, at Halabi, and the mission, and even at Nassien, for being related to the people who owned her like some fancy property.

Nassien must have picked up on Kay's mood. As they stepped through the hatch, she turned around. "Something on your mind?" she asked in Novan.

"Ser, why was the XO questioning my legal status?"

Nassien couldn't look her in the eye. "As a gene line designate, your citizenship is under a different category than a natural-born Novan."

Kay balled her fists. "That's why when you terminate my gene line, you can physically terminate all of us."

Nassien glared at her. "That's why mine is the only military clan that recruits from terminated gene lines to create the Black March, one the most feared and successful Novan military organizations ever created."

From death to death. Kay was supposed to be grateful for that crumb?

Nassien's datapad buzzed. She whipped it out of her pocket and glowered at the screen. "Dismissed!"

Kay marched out of the hatch and let it slam shut behind her, but not before she heard the unmistakable sound of Nassien's datapad being slammed against the bulkhead. She was halfway across the ship before she realized she was missing her MP shadow. Screw it. She was only half a person anyway. She scrambled up the nearest ladder to Deck 2. It was about time she reacquainted herself with her Navy girl and that moonshine rotgut.

Nassien didn't contact her for the rest of day shift, which was good, because Kay spent most of it in a drunken stupor. Hours after she'd worn out her welcome in Naval quarters, she hunted down Jax at his rack.

"What the hell happened to you?" he asked, getting up to make room for her on the rack.

"Nothing." The buzz was wearing off and the unbearable headache already starting. "I think I'm going to be sick."

Jax managed to ram a bucket under her chin before the contents of her stomach came up for a visit. After she heaved her guts out, Jax handed her something to wipe her mouth with.

"Where did you get the booze?"

"Someplace I'll never be allowed back in." The details were vague, but she remembered ranting for a good long time about Nassien, and the military, and Nassien. Her Navy girl gave her the boot in the end. Another enemy to add to the collection. She dropped her head in her hands. "I should have stayed in the brig."

Jax patted her shoulder. "That bad, eh?"

She looked up. "You know they don't even consider us citizens? We're not even human to them."

Jax clenched his jaw. "Yes, I know. Remember, my line is already terminated. Guess I should be grateful Nassien recruited me into the Black March along with Tajex."

"Grateful my ass." Kay grabbed the bucket and heaved some more. Her datapad buzzed in her pocket but she ignored it. It was already going to be a shitty night. She didn't need a summons to make it any worse.

Kay woke up with a splitting headache. She registered that she was in Jax's rack, it was well into ship's night, and her pet MP looked less that happy with her, but she didn't protest when the MP half dragged her back to Nassien's quarters.

She did insist on stopping at one of the other heads to splash cold water on her face. One look in the dull mirror told her she looked as bad as she felt. She ran wet hands through her hair and that settled some of the unruly black mess. At least she hadn't spewed on her uniform. Black showed everything.

The MP walked her back to Nassien's quarters and waited until she keyed open the hatch before leaving. Even at the late hour, the lights were on and Nassien sat at her desk.

She stood up as Kay entered. "Do not leave these quarters again without your MP escort."

So it was back to Terran Standard again? With her hangover, Kay didn't have any fight left in her. "Yes, Ma'am."

Nassien sniffed. "You stink. Take a shower." She stepped through her own hatch and shut it without waiting for Kay's acknowledgment.

One of the benefits of officer quarters was a private shower in the head, and a laundry service. Kay dropped her dirty uniform down the laundry chute and stepped into the shower. After a short but vigorous scrub down, she felt as good as she was going to with the pounding hangover headache. Malik wasn't snoring when she stepped through their hatch, which meant he was awake and keeping his eye on her as usual. Screw him as well. She crawled into her rack and threw the covers over her head.

SHE WOKE UP alone the next morning to the sound of drilling. She glanced at her datapad. One message from ship's store to say her package was ready. She'd had enough sense to place that order before she passed out for the night. Squad training started in the well deck in thirty minutes. She threw on a clean uniform to the sound of that incessant drilling and stepped into the main office. Nassien's hatch was open and that's where the noise was coming from. Were officers subject to fits of redecorating, even on a Navy ship?

Kay ignored the open hatch to Nassien's bunk. She wouldn't be in there anyway. Kay's datapad had a constant overlay now of Nassien's schedule, and she was finishing up a session on the defense grid simulators. Kay picked up her MP escort and made a quick stop at ship's store before proceeding to the lab for suit-up. Her MP left her at the hatch.

Nassien was already there, stripped down to her underwear. The scar on her calf wasn't the only one she had. There was another across her tight stomach. Kay's gaze took in the full package before she came back to her senses and saluted. She handed over the package.

Nassien read the cover and smiled, one replacement executive officer datapad, for the one she'd shattered against the bulkhead. She put it on Huda's lab bench. "Sorry about the construction this morning."

Her aunt glanced between the two of them at the sound of Terran Standard, but didn't say a word.

"What are they building, Ma'am?"

"Another rack. Chumo is returning to duty today." Nassien's grin widened as she pointed to Malik and another man half in their suits already. Chumo was the shorter of the two, with close-cropped hair and a fresh scar that cut through his otherwise bearded chin.

Kay didn't get to ask who was going to bunk in the new rack. She was afraid of the answer, given that Nassien's bodyguards were both male. She suited up, with appropriate checks and double-checks from Huda, and joined the rest of her squad outside the well deck control compartment where one of the Navy specialists waited, along with two other Black March soldiers.

Nassien flexed her arms and legs in the suit and looked around. "Where is Jax and Tajex?" she said over their squad comm-channel.

"Delayed, ser. We were ordered to go ahead with the training session." The speaker looked like any other Black March behemoth but Kay's helmet HUD displayed her identification, rank, and specialization—another fire team gunner, for Jax's fire team.

Nassien glanced around once more and then nodded to the Navy specialist. "Proceed."

The Navy specialist provided the details of this next training session. "The best we can simulate for a high-orbit insertion is to create a high gravity environment in the well deck. We will switch to 4 g along the horizontal axis for optimum drop distance."

Nassien turned to Kay, who was the only one there who hadn't practiced this procedure before. "Trigger your suit's positional jets at least thirty meters before impact on this drill. In the real drop, you'll want them slowing you down around the half-kilometer mark."

Kay nodded. Seemed simple enough, hang at one end of the well deck until the specialist adjusted gravity, and then drop for sixty meters, engage jets, and hope to land in something other than a clump at the end. She bet those jets were going to take some getting used to. She also bet she would be the only one of the six of them who ended up in that ungraceful clump. Where was Jax when she needed someone else to look the fool with her?

The six of them stepped inside the well deck, and the hatch sealed shut behind them. The deck held the Black March ship and a couple of Navy transport shuttles in mechanical lockdown. The destroyed Marine transport had been dismantled and cleared off. That gave them a good one hundred meters of clear space to practice in.

Nassien looped a gloved hand around a pipe. "Hold on to the bulkhead pipes so you don't fall too early."

Kay lined up next to her, with Malik and Chumo on Nassien's other side. The last two lined up beyond Chumo.

"Rotating to position to increase gravity now," The Navy specialist said over the well deck intercom. It took ten minutes to rotate before Kay felt her body floating free. Black March suits were built to protect the owners and instill fear in the enemy. The only thing they instilled while they hung from the pipes as the well deck rotated was an urge to giggle.

They hung like that for another ten minutes. Kay felt no shift in gravity. How long could it take to engage 4 g?

After another five minutes of waiting, Nassien switched on her comm. "Is there a problem, Specialist?"

Kay glanced back to the hatch, but there was no direct visibility into the assembly deck and control compartment from her angle.

Nassien repeated her query on ship's communications.

Kay read her HUD. Something was wrong. She switched to Terran on instinct. "Ma'am, my ship comm link is off."

"So is mine." Nassien switched back to Novan. "Malik, try yours."

Malik lifted his arm in a loose gesture that made no sense, and then he went limp. His grip disengaged from the bulkhead pipe, and he fell.

"Malik!" Nassien tried to grab him as he dropped but he was beyond her reach.

Kay looked down the line. Chumo and the other two soldiers were also dropping like dead wood. "What's wrong?"

"Their suits are either dead or gone into reboot. They'll hit the closed-docking iris but the suit can handle the impact. Avoid them when we drop."

Kay watched them fall. Why all of them? Why not hers or Nassien's?

The answer hit her in an instant. "Someone shut their suits down." She watched them land in a clump on the closed iris that sealed the well deck from space.

Nassien swore and switched to another comm channel that Kay couldn't hear, either. "All comm is dead. Try the hatch."

Kay maneuvered hand over hand to the hatch. She gave the handle a suit-enhanced tug. "No go. It's been locked from the other side." What was the point of this attack, anyway, if it was an attack? The suits protected them whether engaged or rebooting. In five minutes, Malik and the rest would be operational again.

The well deck alarm clamored in her ears a moment later. She'd been on enough transports to recognize that sound. Someone was opening the iris to space at hyper jump speed. Anything not mechanically locked down would be sucked out when that iris opened.

Now she understood the threat.

CHAPTER 11

Gene Study—KDTU-02128 Replicant Status-3069 AH

M. Nassien—Executive override of program manager evaluation on further replicant creation. Approval granted to evaluate stage 5 cloning, to begin in 3070 AH based on profile gene identification on blastocyst. Three-month in vitro survival rate targeted at 60%.

"They'll be pulled out of the ship!" Nassien shouted over the claxon. She started a hand over hand shift as if intending to reach the soldiers.

Kay grabbed hold of her. She dampened external audio in her helmet and flicked on a private channel to Nassien. "So will you. Your suit doesn't have a strong enough mechanical grip to latch on."

She didn't know if her suit was strong enough either, but it was better than Nassien's. She already felt the pull of open space as she slammed Nassien against the bulkhead and wrapped one arm around her. She gave up the bulkhead pipe in favor of holding on to the hatch handle, latching on, and locking her suit's grip to that bar. Her back was to the iris, but the increased pull against her grip told her it was opening up.

Nassien seemed to recognize her weakness finally and wrapped herself around Kay in an embrace that would be questionable in anything other than the massive body armor they both wore. They were helmet to helmet, close enough to see the sweat on Nassien's brow as she watched over Kay's shoulder. Anything not anchored rushed down to the partially opened well deck iris. The pull increased. Kay's HUD registered the strain on her suit to hold on against that force even if she couldn't fully feel it physically.

Nassien shut her eyes, and Kay knew Malik and the others were gone.

Even if his suit came back to life, he and the others had maybe two hours of reserve oxygen. It would take the ship thirty hours to decelerate from hyper-jump speed, not that it would to rescue four soldiers, not even for Nassien.

The well deck alarm stopped. Nassien opened her eyes and looked over Kay's shoulder. "The iris is closing. Someone's here."

Question was, who? And would they finish off what the spacing didn't complete? Kay's HUD tracked the lessening strain on her grip. She didn't know how much more the suit could have handled, and hoped she'd never need to find out. The well deck iris was shut again, but it took another fifteen minutes to normalize pressure. Nassien disengaged from Kay in that time.

Kay didn't let go of her or the hatch handle. "We don't know who opened the iris, or who just shut it." She flicked on her suit armament status. No guns or bullets, and two empty knife sheaths in each wrist. "Damn. I'm empty. How about you?"

"Same. No munitions were required." She pulled up her obsidian blade. "This is it."

"A ceremonial blade? Is it functional?"

Nassien's expression darkened. "Highly functional in the right hands."

The hatch handle moved. Kay switched her grip to a bulkhead pipe and put herself in front of Nassien. Someone had tried to space them all, but she was beginning to believe that Nassien was the real target.

"I'm the armed one," Nassien said.

"And I'm the one armored like a tank." Kay's boots rested on the deck before she remembered to add a belated, "Ma'am."

Kay crouched, ready to barrel through whatever waited for

them. Being a repeat target for death pissed her off, and this suit was going to make sure if their enemies were behind that hatch, she'd take a few of them out along the way. The hatch swung open. A surprised MP stepped back as Kay pushed through and used the bulk of her body armor to stand between Nassien and an army of Navy MPs. None had rifles pointed at her. Behind the MPs were one dead Navy specialist and Nassien's aunt holding a station-safe pistol on a Marine who was flat down on the deck but alive.

"This one didn't get to swallow his suicide pill on time," she said.

Nassien stepped around Kay and tapped her helmet. "Help me off with this thing."

Huda left the Marine with the MPs and unlocked Nassien's helmet. Nassien pulled it off and handed it to her. "How did you know we were in trouble?"

Huda pulled out her datapad. "You think I don't monitor you every time you put on that suit? Your heart rate went through the roof, along with your adrenal levels. When I couldn't pull up the readings from either of your bodyguards, I knew."

Nassien couldn't wipe the tears in her eyes with her gloves on, so Huda did it for her.

"I'm sorry," Huda said. "They were good soldiers. Loyal."

"Yes." Nassien straightened up. She pointed to the Marine. "Isolate him, no chance of self-inflicted harm. I want him interrogated."

"Yes, ser." The lead MP pulled out a hypo and shot the Marine in the arm, knocking him out. Two others carried him off the assembly deck.

Huda wasn't ready to put away her pistol. She stepped up to Kay and unlocked her helmet. "Take it off. I want to see your eyes."

Kay turned at Nassien.

"Aunt, she's okay."

"Helmet off." Huda took a step back. Kay lifted her helmet

off, only to end up facing the business end of Huda's pistol. She froze.

"Put your gun down." Nassien's voice left no option but to comply.

Huda lowered her hand as she stared at Kay, and then shook her head. "I don't know what to say, Ayaan. Those black eyes reveal nothing." She leaned in closer. "Are they real?"

Kay looked away. "Dyed. They are naturally blue."

"Hmm. Blue eyes are just as soulless." Huda turned to Nassien. "Do you trust her?"

Nassien nodded. "You taught me yourself about the sacred sanctity of all life, Aunt. And the honor due to one who saved another. Kay kept me alive in there."

Huda looked back at Kay. "Forgive me. It's been too many years now that someone has been trying to take my niece from me, like they took my brother. It gets harder and harder to recognize an ally."

So her father was killed and Nassien's been hunted for years. So much for the life of the privileged. Nassien stepped to the side to talk with the Navy officer in charge.

Kay took the opportunity to ask the question that had been bugging her for weeks. "Why do they want her dead so bad?"

"Why?" Huda said. "Because she's Nomani and Nassien and there couldn't be two more opposite clans. The Nassiens are military to the core from the highest Novan caste. Nomanis are in the religious caste, against all excuses for violence." She stared at her pistol. "And yet here I am, religious objections discarded to protect my niece. This place, it ruins people."

It really was an outrageous family feud, and yet it was jeopardizing an important mission. How far would they go to eliminate Nassien? Kay looked back at the well deck. Pretty damned far. Still, there had to be easier times to try and kill her than in the middle of deep space.

She turned to the sound of rapidly approaching footfalls.

Jax approached her. "What happened? Are you okay?" He stared up at her, out of breath and only half dressed.

"Someone tried to space us," Kay said. "Where the hell have you been?"

Jax glanced at Nassien's back. "Sickbay. Tajex and I had to carry a soldier there after she passed out in her suit."

"Good thing or you'd have been spaced, too. Someone triggered a remote reboot, then opened the well deck iris." She nodded to Huda. "She's the one who saved us."

Tajex appeared a moment later and reported to Nassien. Kay couldn't hear the exchange, but Tajex didn't look pleased.

Nassien dismissed him and then returned to their group. She didn't waste a glance at Jax. "Suits off. Training is done until Tajex can reform the squad."

She marched off with Huda at her side and one of Kay's MP bodyguards in tow. Kay shrugged at Jax and followed.

Huda didn't put down her pistol until they were locked in the lab with the MP outside the hatch. It was a long process to get out of the suit, and she helped Nassien first. Nassien's stoic act disintegrated before she was fully out of the suit. She leaned over in the suit bay, hands covering her face as she sobbed. Huda patted her shoulders while Kay wished for all the world that she still had her helmet on and could at least pretend not to overhear it all.

"They've been with me since I turned seventeen. Five years."

"It's not your fault," Huda said.

Nassien straightened and brushed Huda's hand away. "And whose fault is it then? My father, my cousin, these two, how many have to die just because I was born?"

Kay's thoughts latched on to a different track, anything to pull Nassien out of her downward spiral, even if she didn't understand the half of it. She broke Nassien's rule and spoke Novan, for Huda's sake. "Respectfully, ser. It may not just be you they are after."

Nassien wiped an angry hand across her face, as if she'd just remembered Kay's presence. "You think this was Mr. Halabi? Seems an elaborate plot to eliminate one individual from a gene line."

"Halabi?" Huda asked, her eyes widening.

Nassien waved her off. "I'll explain later."

"That's my point, though, ser. If you were the sole target, why kill twenty or more soldiers and ground the Marine company? And why bring in a Terran spy?"

Huda glared at her.

"Another Terran, Aunt," Nassien said. "So you think it's the gene bank they are after?"

"Probably both. This attack, regardless of the others, was aimed at you, Ayaan." Huda tapped Nassien's suit leggings. "Let me get you out of this first, then you can discuss possibilities."

Kay cooled her heels as she waited her turn, but her mind still raced over the assassination attempt. It wasn't going to help her reputation with the Navy XO that she was involved in yet another "incident."

Nassien pulled on her uniform while Huda worked on Kay's suit. She unlatched the gloves, then the arms and torso, and locked them into the suit bay. The legs took longer, but eventually, Kay was left to pull off the bodysuit and get back into her black uniform.

Nassien sat on a bench with her head in her hands while Huda shut down the last of her equipment. Kay stood to the side, wishing she could disappear into the bulkhead if Nassien's mood was shifting back again.

Nassien looked up at her, and Kay snapped to attention. "Oh just sit down, would you?"

Kay sat on the opposite bench. The strain on Nassien was obvious, but it wasn't something officers were supposed to show in front of the grunts, and Kay didn't know how to react. Huda patted Nassien's shoulder, then disappeared through a hatch to another section of the lab. Nassien dropped her head into her hands again, only this time, the unmistakable shake of her shoulders said she was crying, again.

Kay stiffened. Officers don't cry. That wasn't in the regs. She looked at the hatch where Huda disappeared. No rescue was coming from that direction. Nassien's shoulders still shook, but no sound escaped that Kay could hear. It didn't matter, though. The pheromone shift was obvious. Kay never could protect herself against a crying woman.

Shit.

She moved to Nassien's bench and placed an awkward hand on her back. Nassien leaned into her, sobbing quietly. Kay stayed in that strained position until Huda returned and glared at her through narrowed eyes until Kay stood up at attention, again.

Nassien wiped her eyes as she glanced between Kay and Huda, then she shook her head and laughed.

"You're a target already, Ayaan. This would make it worse," Huda said, waving a hand at Kay.

Nassien's expression hardened, and she stood up. "I have a prisoner to interrogate."

"With no guards?"

Nassien's hand beat a hard rhythm against her leg, and then she turned to Kay.

Huda stepped closer. "No."

Nassien ignored her and pulled out her obsidian knife. Kay didn't flinch, but sank to her knees. The sound of Nassien's oath barely penetrated her thoughts, with words of ritual, obligation, and legal nuances that she couldn't begin to comprehend yet. What was important was the end, where Nassien made Huda hand over her station-safe pistol to Kay.

"See the Master-at-Arms for a replacement." Nassien walked to Malik's gear. After a pause, she opened his locker and rummaged around. She pulled out two knives and a wrist sheath.

Kay checked the gun for adequate ammunition and holstered it, then slid one of Malik's knives into her boot and strapped on the wrist sheath. The act was done. She was Nassien's bodyguard. It put a bigger bull's-eye on her head, but at least she was armed enough to defend herself now. Nassien stepped out the hatch, and Kay followed, leaving Huda to stew on her own. They picked up Kay's MP and made their way across the ship and up a level to the brig.

They stepped through a hatch to a different set of compartments in the brig than Kay had seen on her last visit. In one, the prisoner was strapped on a table, surrounded by an odd assortment of instruments and needles. This wasn't going to be pleasant.

She stood silent sentinel behind Nassien, with the MP outside, as the interrogation began. Her stomach nearly revolted after the first few tools were put to use and the screaming started, but Nassien kept her face neutral as she asked question after question between each application of pain.

After two hours, the prisoner broke. Unfortunately, he wasn't that well informed, but he did point out two co-conspirators who were then brought in for "questioning." First shift dragged on through second shift and into third. Nassien remained stiff-backed through the whole process, listening, questioning, and hypothesizing. In the end, three more Marines, five Navy personnel, and one Black March soldier were in the brig awaiting court martial and execution.

Back in their quarters, Nassien leaned against her desk with dark circles under her eyes. "Opinions?"

Kay stood at ease. "We may or may not have neutralized the threat to you, but we still don't have the original bombers who took out the mess hall and Marine transport."

"Assuming it wasn't Ysabet."

"Even if it was," which Kay still struggled to believe, "someone had to have worked with her. You have a confession from the Black March soldier who supplied the explosive material, but not from anyone who created the bombs. And why bother with either explosion if they were after you? There remain two targets to this operation, you, and the mission overall."

"Don't you think you are a target as well? Someone's tried to kill you at least twice now."

Kay shrugged. "There's never a lot of trust for the Terran in the squad." And there would be less now that she was one of the few people on ship who was armed, for whatever reason.

Nassien flinched. She raised a hand toward Kay, and then dropped it back to her side. "Unaltered Terran gene line integration into active duty is a rare occurrence. Unfortunately it's never a smooth transition."

Kay shrugged. "So I noticed. The main focus remains on you—your life, your mission."

"And Halabi."

"And Halabi. Question is, why is he out to get you, and is he crazy enough to risk everything to take you out and let the Terrans get the gene bank?"

Nassien sat at her chair, staring at the blank console for a long time. She looked up at Kay. "I don't know. My grandmother had his family removed from the Nassien inner circle, but I don't know why. It all happened before I was born."

"What about your mother and father? Could he be trying to get back at them for something, through you?"

"I can't think of a reason. My father died before I was born, around the same time as my grandfather. Other than the transgression of having a child with a Nomani, my mother has been a model officer for decades."

Nassien's tone spoke volumes about how little regard she had for that model officer mother.

"What about that Nomani connection?" Kay asked. "Your aunt suggested that was reason enough to be a target."

Nassien's jaw tightened. "I'm not the first half-caste child to be born."

Now that hit a nerve. Kay let the argument go, but felt Huda was closer to the truth than Nassien wanted to believe. Hell, if Nomanis were pacifists, it could be one of them taking that stance to an extreme because Nassien had embraced her military family instead of them.

Nassien rubbed her already bloodshot eyes. "The case goes

to the Navy's chief interrogator tomorrow. I'll be informed of any important updates, but I don't expect we'll learn much more. I need sleep."

Kay moved toward the hatch where she'd bunked with Malik, but Nassien but a hand on her arm. "Your gear was moved to my compartment. Chumo . . ."

Nassien couldn't finish but Kay understood. Chumo was supposed to reclaim his rack today. She visited the head first, and then followed Nassien through the other hatch. The compartment was bigger than the one she'd shared with Malik. This was where Nassien kept her personal items. Kay tried to take it in with an unobtrusive glance, from the prayer rug rolled up in a corner, to the elaborate Mecca clock, and a shelf of what she assumed were family photos.

She turned away from it all to face the double bunk. "Are you top or bottom?"

Nassien quirked an eyebrow. "Top, definitely."

Kay bit back a reply that would only land her in trouble. It would be hard enough bunking with Nassien as it was. While Nassien was out at the head, Kay stripped to her tank top and boxers and crawled into the bottom rack. She contemplated stuffing a knife under her pillow but gave up that idea. The hatch had a manual latch that would take a blowtorch to cut through from the outside, and Nassien had ordered the two sworn Navy MPs to alternate guard outside the hatch.

Kay shut her eyes when Nassien returned a few minutes later. She kept them shut while Nassien shuffled around the small compartment, but curiosity got the better of her when she heard the soft, rhythmic cadence of Nassien's voice. Peeking through half-lidded eyes, she saw Nassien in profile on her prayer mat. Kay couldn't follow the words as they were not in standard Novan, but in some older, religious language. She closed her eyes and didn't dare move until Nassien finished. She opened her eyes when the chanting ended.

Nassien placed her mat back in the corner and turned to Kay. Her expression wasn't quite peaceful, but definitely less strained than it was a few minutes ago. She smiled at Kay and hoisted herself into the upper bunk. Kay watched the lean brown legs disappear above her before shutting her eyes again.

Sleep didn't come for a long time after that.

NASSIEN DETOURED TO the training classes three days later with Kay at her heels. Kay's presence as an armed guard hadn't gone well with the Navy XO, and a vein in Tajex's head popped out whenever he saw her in meetings, but the rest of the command staff didn't seem to care. She didn't think she'd be as lucky with her own peers. She opened the hatch to see Tajex presenting test results to the mixed squads that had been drilling together.

Nassien interrupted his presentation and pulled him outside the hatch. "I need replacements for Malik and Chumo's place in this mission. Who do you recommend to fill out the command squad?"

Tajex led Nassien to the side. Kay kept her in sight but tried to give her the same level of discrete surveillance that she'd seen Malik do.

Jax stepped through the hatch, and his gaze locked onto the holster strapped to her thigh. "What are you doing with a pistol?"

She nodded toward Nassien. "Guard duty."

He pulled her to the side. "No. You can't. She's going to get you killed."

She glanced at him, then back to Nassien. "I don't need her help in that area."

"This isn't a joke, Kay. She's not going to live through this mission. You know that."

She gave him a hard look. "What do you know?"

He took a step back. "Everyone knows. If you ever got out of her shadow, you'd know, too. There isn't a soldier here who doesn't realize someone's got it in for Nassien, someone with more power than she has."

Kay eyed up the mingled group of Black March and ex-Marines visible through the open hatch. Who else was a traitor? Would she recognize the next attack when it came?

"This isn't you," Jax whispered. "I don't know what kind of hold she's got on you, but break out of it. This is not the mission you want to take a stand on."

Nassien returned, and Kay fell in place behind her, but Jax's warning rang in her ears. She hadn't resisted when Nassien initiated her with the Knife Oath. Hell, she'd volunteered. He was right, that wasn't her style.

One deep inhale of Nassien's scent, and Kay knew exactly what kind of hold the woman had on her, and it was her own damned fault. She volunteered for that as well, letting personal feelings override self-preservation. She rested a hand on her holstered pistol. The perks made up for it though, given that she was already a target on this mission. At least she had a weapon and a legitimate reason to use it. Question was, how far would she go to keep Nassien alive versus protect her own hide?

Nassien led her up two decks and keyed a hatch on Deck 1 that Kay had been to only once before. They stepped into a small compartment dominated by a blank wide-screen display, a biometric head cap, and gloves made of the same material as the Black March body suit they wore inside the exoskeleton. Kay recognized it all from her targeting simulation test.

Nassien took the seat in front of the display and flicked a few controls. The screen came alive, showing a rocky, snow-covered terrain of high mountains and deep gullies.

She turned to Kay. "This simulates the gene bank defense grid. You used it in your targeting test. Unfortunately, I am the one who rated high enough on the tests to manage the defense grid, if necessary."

"I want you to pay close attention, both to the assumed Terran tactics and my responses. I need you to think about possible alternatives, anything that would give either us or the Terrans a tactical advantage."

"Yes, Ma'am."

Nassien pulled on the head cap and gloves and turned back to the display. Kay didn't see her hit any other controls, but the display filled in with a Terran bomber group and a full squadron of attack helicopters as cover to an infantry battalion. Nassien twitched her gloved fingers, and four gun turrets emerged from the snow banks to tear through the Terran line. Target images flashed faster than Kay could follow as Nassien reacted to each shift in Terran tactics.

It was a long two hours before Nassien pulled herself out of the simulator. She looked haggard as she took off the head cap and gloves.

"Are you okay?" Kay asked.

Nassien rubbed her temples. "The grid takes full advantage of Novan multitasking enhancements. I can operate it for a time, but the assigned operators are specially bred for the task. I assume they avoid the kind of headache I have now." She lowered her hands. "What did you get out of that?"

Kay shrugged. "I couldn't follow most of it. The Terran tactics were biased toward a broad-based infantry attack. How does the grid hold up to sustained air attack that could target the gun turrets?"

Nassien slumped in her chair. "Well enough with a trained operator. The guns are on rails that can randomize their locations better than I just did. I'll have the simulation reprogrammed to include that option."

"Ma'am, is there a backup for you?" Kay meant it as a suggestion to dump the task on someone else.

"In case I don't make it?" Nassien took a different meaning. "No, there isn't. Yours was the next highest test results, but long-term exposure would cause you permanent brain damage. My need to engage the grid is theoretical anyway if the site is intact when we arrive." She let out a long sigh and stood up. "The platoon commanders are waiting to give their readiness updates. We drop in-system in two days."

Those final two days were a blur of meetings that

threatened to bore Kay to death. Pre-mission jitters were present throughout the ship, from Navy, to Marines who were no longer idle, to the Black March, who had yet to gel as a cohesive fighting force. It looked to be one of the rockiest missions Kay had ever participated in. It didn't help that Jax was turning into a stranger, and she had no real free time to slap him back into place. Nassien dominated all her time now that she was her sworn guard.

The Navy XO had a special glower for Kay every time they met, and that didn't change when she and Nassien joined him on the quarterdeck for the transition to normal space. It was second shift, but the first shift Navy officers Kay recognized from the endless meeting hell were present. She knew as many Navy faces now as she did Marine and Black March.

Kay and Nassien were the only non-Navy personnel present.

The XO saluted Nassien, then turned to his controls. "Call general quarters."

His comm officer repeated the order, calling the Navy personnel to battle-ready status. It was a long shot that they'd transition into an immediate threat, but safety required they be ready. She knew the Marines and Black March would be on edge as well. Nothing was worse than shipping in knowing you were useless until you got dirt side.

The Navy captain joined them from a side hatch. She was gray-haired, short-tempered, and the only officer on board who outranked Nassien. She accepted Nassien's salute with a grunt and took her seat. "Carry on Mr. Moki."

The XO walked through a long series of commands, echoed by his officers and carried out in various departments throughout the ship. Kay swallowed hard to avoid a repeat of her last meal when the ship finally made the transition out of hyper jump. She glanced at the view screens, but saw nothing except a few pinpoints of light.

"Status," Mr. Moki said.

Reports came in one department at a time. Nassien waited

on the balls of her feet. The same tension radiated through her as well. There was only one report the two of them were waiting for and it came in twenty minutes in-system.

"Ser, registering three Terran ships. Two troop transports and one drone-class battleship."

"Range."

"Eight light-minutes."

Far enough away that they had hours of deceleration time and in-system cruising before they'd be in range of each other's weapons.

"And our ships?"

"No sign yet."

CHAPTER 12

Gene Study—KDTU-02128 Replicant Status-3070 AH

Stage 5 status changed to Priority 1 Experimental, replicant creation program accelerated per order of M. Nassien, designated Gen 5 Crèche G, with funding for three experimentals. Protest lodged by Project Manager that no replicants to date have proven out their gene line target of exceptional situational awareness and tactical ability. In the absence of such result, targeted gene isolation cannot be established. Protest registered and acknowledged, but overridden by authority of M. Nassien. Gene set manipulation to proceed based on secondary classified gene set identification from Gen 4 Crèche F.

The XO accepted the report without comment, but Kay saw his eyes twitch toward them.

Nassien stepped forward. "I want full stats on all three ships. We'll meet in Tactical at your convenience, Mr. Moki."

"Yes, ser."

She saluted the C.O. and stepped into the passageway. Kay followed. Their own ships would arrive soon. Navy transports were first as they were the slowest and needed more time to decelerate and maneuver into position. Given the distance from their transition point to planetary orbit and the Terran ships, it would be a long deceleration.

Two hours later they joined the XO and platoon commanders for a debriefing. Kay took up her position behind Nassien's seat. The benefit of being the new bodyguard was that she could now stare down anyone who glared at her. A threat to her was a threat to Nassien. They all knew it and hated it. It was the only fun she got in this new gig.

The XO turned on the display. It showed a close-up of the Chagos Belt, with red dots for the enemy ships. "We have three enemy ships entrenched in-system. We can't tell how long they've been here, and it will be another ten hours before our recon drones report on ground status at the mines and the gene bank."

"What are the specs on those three ships?" Nassien asked.

The XO switched the display to a stream of specifications. "One is the *Norfolk*, transport for the 23rd Armored battalion. Given its current position in the shadow of the battleship, it has likely already landed troops and equipment on the mining colony. The other transport is the *Volga*, capable of carrying two mechanized infantry companies. It's currently in a neutral position in-system, so its status is unclear. The battleship is the *Rubicon*. It carries four attack squadrons and a full drone wing. It's armed with two primary batteries of plasma cannons and a secondary battery laser gun. It's also near the mining colony and likely engaging with in-system defenses."

Nassien nodded. "That will likely occupy our Legion-class carrier and one of the battle cruisers when they arrive."

The XO raised his hand for silence while he listened to his ear comm. "Our second troop transport just arrived in-system."

"Good. They can support the Marines on the mining operation. That leaves us and one battle cruiser to bolster the defenses at the gene bank. Given the position of the *Rubicon*, the Terrans are focused on the mines. Our initial battle plan remains, contingent on the ground reports we get in ten hours. We'll launch the Black March shuttle with the Marines while this ship makes a high-orbit flyover to insert the Black March troops over the gene bank facility."

The XO glared at Kay. "That tactic leaves us vulnerable to both the *Volga's* armaments and any surface-to-air missiles they have on the ground."

"Risk noted, Mr. Moki. Please continue."

The XO looked like he'd swallowed something nasty, but he didn't contradict Nassien's plan. He proceeded with a rundown of all the equipment and firepower the Terrans likely had, based on the Novan data on the three ships. Kay only half-listened. Most of the details would be up to the other three inbound Novan ships. The only thing she needed to hear was the ground reports, and they weren't coming for another ten hours.

Nassien spent three-and-a-half hours getting reports from each platoon commander before finally heading back to their quarters. With less than five hours before they had to be up for the ground reports, Kay hit the rack and fell asleep without a second thought.

Less than five hours later, she woke up to the sound of Nassien pacing their tiny space. Three steps, turn. Three steps, turn. Kay rolled the other way, but she couldn't block out that nervous cadence.

She rolled back and stuck her head out. "Is there a problem, Ma'am?"

Nassien stopped in her tracks. "A problem? You mean other than ordering over two hundred soldiers into what could be their deaths? No. No problem."

Kay sat up and rubbed her eyes, then flicked on the lights. Nassien was still in uniform. So much for sleep. She didn't know if she had it in her to give a pep talk to a nervous officer. "Respectfully, Ma'am, you're an officer. That is your job to call the mission."

"And is yours to die?"

"If the mission calls for it."

Nassien flinched.

Maybe someone would miss her if she bought it on this one, someone besides Jax anyway. She studied Nassien's face. There was something more there, something she recognized from other squad mates.

She lowered her head in her hands. This can't be happening. She took a deep breath and looked back up. "This is your first mission." She didn't bother making it a question. She recognized that scared newbie look. There was green, and there was who let you out of military school?

For a moment Nassien's officer facade slipped, and Kay got a good long look at sheer fright before the mask returned in the form of an icy glare.

"Go back to sleep." Nassien flicked off the light and stepped out of the hatch to her desk.

Kay rolled back into her rack, but sleep wasn't coming as quickly this time. A sabotaged mission with a green commanding officer. She might bite it on this mission after all.

"GROUND REPORT, MR. Moki," Nassien rasped. She wore the same uniform with a few more creases. Dark circles under her eyes announced how little sleep she'd gotten. Kay noted every person in the room—a good portion of the platoon commanders, including Tajex—reacted to Nassien's less-than-pristine state.

The XO cleared his throat. "We have two reports, ser. I'd like to start with the *Rubicon*. It started shifting position three hours ago, when our battle cruisers arrived in-system."

"Is it coming out to intercept the cruisers?"

"No. Its speed and trajectory suggest it is moving to cover the transport, which is also shifting toward the gene bank. Based on this, we have re-evaluated planetary deployment of your troops."

Nassien glared at him. "I did not authorize a change in plans."

The XO couldn't hide a triumphant smirk. He was enjoying this. "The C.O. has communicated with the captains of both battle cruisers to coordinate tactical adjustments based on the *Rubicon*."

Nassien pushed her chair back hard enough to slam the bulkhead behind her as she stood up. This was it, she was going to commit career suicide, and Kay wasn't going to have to lift a finger to make Halabi's wish come true.

Halabi was an asshole. So was the XO, just waiting for Nassien to pop. Another rule Kay lived by popped into her head. Assholes shouldn't win.

She switched on her subvocalizer. "Ma'am."

"What?" Nassien glared at her.

Kay came up with the fastest excuse she could think of and spoke aloud in Novan. "Ser, Huda is requesting your immediate attention."

Nassien frowned. "Can't this wait?"

Kay knew she picked the right person to break Nassien's concentration. "Sorry, ser, she said it was mission-critical."

Nassien continued to frown at her, but Kay kept herself steady and relaxed. Either Nassien took the bait or didn't. There wasn't much else Kay could do besides drag her physically from the meeting until she calmed down.

Nassien turned back to the XO. "We will continue this discussion." She turned on her heel and marched out.

Kay followed silently in her footsteps, wondering what the hell she was going to do once they reached Huda's lab. Nassien wasn't paying any attention to her, so she flicked on her datapad and sent Huda an urgent message that they were on their way.

Huda met them outside the hatch to her lab and led them inside. "What's happened?"

Nassien walked to a bench and sat down. "Isn't that what you're supposed to be telling me?" Huda gave her a blank look, and Nassien turned to Kay with an icy glare. "Explain," she said in Terran.

"You needed a break, Ma'am." Kay switched to Novan for Huda's sake. "You were about to pick a fight with the XO that you could only lose in the end. The battlefield's changed. We need to adapt to that."

"You overstep yourself," Nassien growled.

Kay glared back at her. "You were about to hand Halabi your career on a platter."

Nassien stood up. "You're dismissed."

"How can you dismiss me? I'm your bodyguard."

Nassien stepped up to her. She held Kay's gaze with cold, dark eyes as she pulled the gun out of Kay's holster and tossed it to Huda. "Not anymore." She stepped out of the hatch and kicked it shut behind her.

CHAPTER 13

Gene Study—KDTU-02128 Replicant Status-3075 AH

Crèche F officer training program cancelled after psychological evaluation of replicants revealed deep-seated resentments to official chain-of-command operation. Five replicants from Crèche F transferred to Marine boot camp. Replicant 1 (R1) to serve out six-month sentence for aggravated assault before transfer to Infantry. Active duty to begin within the year. Gene line assigned to Program Manager Benyan Halabi (formerly Nassien. Reference Nassien vs. Nassien, Civil Case 412855-3055 AH).

Kay slammed her fist into the closed hatch, and then let out a stream of obscenities as she cradled that fist to her chest.

Huda stepped closer and held out her hand. "Did you break it?"

"What difference does it make now?" Kay pulled Malik's knives out of her boot and wrist sheath with her good hand and threw them on the bench.

Huda took her hand. Kay clenched her jaw while she examined the damage.

"No, not broken, but you'll need a bandage over those scrapes." Huda went to the first aid kit and came back with ointment and a bandage. She made quick work of wrapping Kay's hand. "That will do. Now you need to get back to your assignment."

"Didn't you listen? I don't have one anymore." Kay flexed her fingers, and then winced. Bad move.

"You accepted the oath. You can't be dismissed from that." Huda grabbed her by the shoulders. "She needs you. She's alone here. And now she's unguarded. What did that oath mean to you? What does she mean to you?" She held out the gun.

Kay holstered it and swung the hatch open. She tried to flick open her datapad with her bandaged hand, but that wasn't worth the pain. She didn't need it anyway. It was just before lunch, and she knew where Nassien would be. She hurried down the passageways, gritting her teeth every time some moron bumped into her bad hand. When she reached Deck 2, she broke into a run. Why was the ship so damned big?

She was out of breath by the time she slapped her palm on the hatch lock to Nassien's quarters. To her surprise, it opened for her. Good to know she hadn't been locked out yet. She rushed inside and stopped short at the open hatchway to their shared racks.

Nassien lay prostrate on her prayer mat. Kay recognized a pause in the normal chanting. She'd been noticed at any rate. She stood at ease just inside the hatch and stared into the blank bulkhead opposite her. She managed to get her breathing under control by the time Nassien rolled up her mat and turned to her, taking in the holstered gun with a glance. Kay kept her eyes averted, just in case. A little humble pie wouldn't hurt her.

Nassien took two steps to close the gap between them. She lifted Kay's chin until they were eye to eye, then pressed her back into the bulkhead with a searing kiss. Kay grabbed a fistful of Nassien's uniform with her good hand when Nassien tried to pull back. She let the passion and the pheromones crash over her and have free rein. At the end, she found herself out of breath, again.

Nassien rested her cheek on Kay's head. Kay was tall, but Nassien was a good few centimeters taller. "Your whole gene line has this problem, you know."

"What problem?"

Nassien took a step back. "None of you take orders well."

Kay shrugged. "We follow the good ones."

One graceful eyebrow quirked upward. "I'll have that added to your psych profile when this mission is over."

Thoughts of the mission brought Kay back to reality. They'd be hitting dirt in less than a day.

Nassien stepped around her to get to the desk console. "All ships are in-system now. I need you to see this."

Kay followed and leaned over her shoulder to read the console report. It was a report from the *Aziz*. The Novan Legion-class carrier had arrived.

Nassien sat down. "Their TAC officer confirms the *Rubicon* is heading for the gene bank."

"Ground conditions are the same. The *Rubicon* is there to prevent us from landing."

Nassien watched her closely. "What are our options?"

Kay stared at the screen. "Scroll down." She pointed with her bandaged hand.

Nassien noticed the bandage. She held it gently in her own for a moment. "Do I want to know how you got this?"

"Got into a scuffle with a hatch. It won this round."

Nassien brushed her fingers along Kay's fingertips. The movement it caused hurt like hell but Kay didn't say a word. Nassien let go and scrolled the *Aziz*'s report.

Kay read the full analysis, and then straightened up. "They can't take the gene bank from space. If we trust Intel, they don't have the right armaments to even make a significant impact once we're on the ground, except for those target drones. They can cause some problems."

"But how do we get to the ground with that between us and the gene bank?"

Kay stared at the bulkhead for a long time, pondering that problem. Then she smiled. "Transfer us to the *Aziz*. Have them take a close-orbit turn around the *Rubicon*, and then we drop on their blind side."

Nassien inhaled sharply. "That's a big risk. If the *Rubicon* outmaneuvers the *Aziz*, we'd either be stranded on the carrier, or dropped too high in orbit for our oxygen to survive until landfall."

"That's a problem for the *Aziz*."

Nassien's datapad buzzed. She read the message out loud. "Ship to ship tactical conference in twenty minutes." She looked back to Kay. "We will need the Marines with us if the Terrans have landed in force. This ship's C.O. won't let her precious tank get in the *Rubicon*'s line of fire, but your tactic will work for them as well. We'll move the Marine company to one of the cruisers and fly them in at the first available window on the cruiser's shuttles."

"Those are unarmed."

Nassien grinned back at her. "Not if we keep the cruiser with them into high orbit. The *Chavez* is a Medina-class, capable of sustained atmospheric conditions. The cruiser can target any significant Terran ground installations as well."

The plan left the mining operations covered only by the second troop transport, but that would have to suffice until they repelled the gene bank attack. That took priority.

Kay followed Nassien into the exec communications compartment for the ship-to-ship tactical review. The Navy C.O., XO Moki, and Marine commander were already seated around a semicircle table. They faced a bank of screens that had the name of each ship highlighted at the bottom. Only the *Aziz* mattered. Convince them, and the rest would follow. The *Aziz* captain was onscreen, young for her command, with a long nose and close-set eyes.

Nassien took control of the meeting from the start. "We all agree that the gene bank is the first priority for the Nassien Autonomy."

It was Kay's idea to cash in on the name. As a member of the ruling family, it would bring all eyes to Nassien and to the presumed ramifications if they countermanded her strategy. Even Kay knew you didn't piss off a Nassien without risking more than just your career.

Nassien tapped her datapad. An overview of their strategy pinged on every local datapad in the meeting and for each C.O. and XO on the remote ships. "I will forward the complete plan shortly, but as you see in the overview, we have an approach to the gene bank that will provide us the ground troops we need to control the facility."

"You risk two Navy ships in this plan," Mr. Moki said. "If we stick with my proposal, *Aziz* and *Chavez* can concentrate their firepower on the *Rubicon* from a safer distance."

"And leave the gene bank to whatever Terran forces are on the ground. The site is protected from air attack but not a sustained ground assault, especially if the Terrans are willing to sustain massive casualties," Nassien said.

Moki shook his head. "With respect, ser, Naval tactics are not your responsibility."

"But the primary target is, and that target is on the ground, Mr. Moki, not in space." Nassien leaned back in her chair. "But you are correct, my proposal is a strategy that can save that target. It is up to the Navy to turn that strategy into tactical advantage and a viable mission."

"The *Chavez* is capable of the high-orbit maneuvers you suggest," the captain of the cruiser said—a silver-haired man with a broad mustache and beard. "We have broadside cannons that can protect the Marine shuttle and ourselves if the *Aziz* can keep the *Rubicon's* drones occupied. If the *Aziz* drops in your Black March and then maneuvers away, we can come in on the *Rubicon's* planet-side flank and attack from both sides while the Marines ship out."

All eyes turned to the captain of the *Aziz*. Her eyes were down, presumably reading Nassien's overview. She looked to Nassien. "Mr. Moki is correct, the proposal does increase the risk to both ships."

"Exactly," Moki said.

Nassien's hand started its rapid tap-tap-tap against her leg. Kay held her breath, but Nassien kept quiet.

"Exactly," the captain of the Aziz said. "But we aren't here to protect the paint on our shiny toys. We are here to ensure the safety of the Novan genome, above all else. Ms. Nassien Nomani's plan has merit."

Kay let out a long, slow breath. It took two more hours of haggling to work out the details with all the ship captains, but Kay and Nassien's strategy was finally approved with only minor alterations.

They had six hours before they had to suit up and transfer to the *Aziz*. The Black March troops were ordered to their racks for the last rest they'd get. Kay led Nassien to her bunk, and they came together in a clash of desperate passion that for a little while, blocked out the danger they were about to face. After a time, they slept in a tangle of arms and legs on the bottom rack.

HUDA SUITED THEM up. Kay walked through a suit-check of armaments. It was the first time she'd be fully loaded. She had her multi-ammo rifle strapped across one shoulder, grenade launcher snapped in place on the other, and a subcompact machine gun in a compartment on her right thigh.

She picked up one of Malik's knives and contemplated bringing it along. It was a weak weapon compared to the rest of her arsenal, but the suit had a built-in wrist sheath.

Nassien walked to her, already encased in her gray suit. She pulled her obsidian knife out of its sheath and exchanged it for the knife Kay held. "This will cut through anything, including a Black March suit. Your wrist sheath is a launcher."

"Then shouldn't you keep it?"

Nassien smiled. "You're better at keeping me alive."

Kay recognized what was unsaid in all this. Terrans weren't their only problem. They still had a shared enemy on this mission, and it could be one of the Black March. She snapped the knife into place. Huda watched them both with a wary eye, but said nothing. Kay wondered if that was Nassien's doing or not. Huda followed them to the shuttles that had arrived to take them all, including technicians, to the *Aziz*.

Jax and Tajex waited for them, along with the fourth member of their fire team, Valderrama.

Kay flicked on a private channel to him. "Looks like you lose your bet."

"You're not ground-side yet," he said.

There was something oddly comforting about having that jackass around again. At least he'd never deliberately tried to kill her. That had to count for something. The other four members of their command squad joined them in the jammed cattle car that took them to the *Aziz*. It was a cargo shuttle, the only ship capable of holding multiple soldiers in full exoskeleton gear.

Kay glanced at the other members of the command squad. They were all original Black March, hand-picked by Tajex, and she didn't recognize any of them. She positioned herself between the strangers and Nassien and flicked on a channel to Jax. "How'd you get Valderrama in our squad?"

"Seemed like a good idea since we've been a team for years already. Tajex agreed." He looked over Kay's shoulder at Nassien who was blocked from their private conversation. "Are you two still attached at the hip?" He turned back when she didn't answer right away. "Shit, you are sleeping with her. Is that why someone tried to space you both?"

"I wasn't sleeping with her back then." Kay held on as the shuttle lurched forward. A bunch of Black March suits slamming around wouldn't hurt them or the suits, but would make for an embarrassing mess to separate when they docked on the *Aziz*.

"But you are now. Dumb move, Kay."

"I know." He was right, it was going to get her killed, but she wasn't turning her back on Nassien now.

He kept silent for the rest of the short trip, until they docked, then he turned the private channel back on. "We watch out for each other. That's what we do, right?"

"Yeah."

"Then take my advice. Someone still has a bull's-eye on her chest, and it doesn't have to be you. It's going to be a wild trip planet-side from orbit. People can get separated, like maybe you and your new friend."

He didn't say anything else as they disembarked, but Kay got the hint. He was betting someone was still after Nassien and wanted her to not be in the line of fire when it happened.

"Sorry, Jax," she said to the closed channel. She was sticking with Nassien to the end.

THEIR TIME ON the *Aziz* dragged on long enough to get on Kay's nerves. Jax was his usual nervous wreck before a mission, but it was Tajex he turned to for idle chatter, not her this time. Even Valderrama was keeping his gibes to a minimum.

High-orbit insertion at night, planet-side in Black March exoskeletons wasn't going to be a thrill ride for any of the ex-Marines. Nassien spent most of the time receiving tactical updates that she shared with Tajex as company commander, the platoon commanders, and privately with Kay. It would likely burn his experimental Tarquin ass if he knew Nassien was keeping her in the loop on everything. He hadn't two words to say to her since the airlock incident. Maybe he was in the same camp as the XO, thinking she was the catalyst for it all.

The ground situation wasn't changing, but other things were. After the final relayed update, Tajex opened a public channel. "The *Aziz* is engaging the enemy. We will drop out of the aft airlock by squad in twenty minutes."

In other words, it was going to be a bumpy ride.

Huda did a final check on Kay's suit, verifying everything from the oxygen tanks to internal life function regulators.

"Nothing's changed since we suited up," Kay said.

"Shut up. Arrogant damned military brat."

It wasn't just the ex-Marines with a bad case of pre-mission jitters.

Huda found something worth tweaking. Kay stood still until Huda gave a final thumbs up. "Stay alive. Keep her alive."

Kay nodded. It was the same plan she had for every

mission. Stay alive, keep Jax alive. And now, keep Nassien alive as well. Everything else was background noise. The first resonating boom took them by surprise as it vibrated through each of them. There was no mistaking the second boom as the *Aziz* fired its cannons a second time. There was also no mistaking the hull rattle when it took its first hit.

Nassien stepped up to her as the squads lined up outside the airlock. "We're showing broadside until we get into position for the drop. The Terrans will take full advantage of that large a target, but the armor will hold."

True to her prediction, the *Aziz* took multiple hits during the fifteen minutes until it rotated between the Terran carrier and the planet.

On cue, every soldier got their first dose of mood enhancers from the suit. Even knowing it was an artificial stimulant didn't change its effect. Kay felt great, ready for anything, though not reckless. She had to give credit to the Novan Psych researchers, they knew exactly which buttons to push and when with these suits. The nervous mood disappeared all around her. Even Jax gave her a thumbs-up.

The first squad filed into the airlock. Kay had no visuals on the result, but she watched Nassien's subtle nod as each squad dropped. As command squad, they were the last to step into the airlock, and it took ages. Kay was ready to roll. In theory, it was much like the spacing attack. The hatch would open and they'd be sucked out in the ship's wake, tiny spears cutting through the upper atmosphere that would be unnoticeable to the *Rubicon*.

Reality wasn't much like theory. She stepped into the air lock with the rest of the command squad. When the hatch opened, she tumbled out of the air lock in a ball instead of the vertical spear she was supposed to be. They were dropping on the dark side of the planet, so there wasn't much on visuals, but her HUD flashed warning beacons at her as she spun.

"Straighten out. Your boot jets will take care of the rest," Nassien said through a private channel.

Kay pulled her arms to her side, forced herself into a line, and triggered the flight controls that ran parallel to her boots. Her body fell into alignment with the fall. She still didn't feel quite oriented. "I'm dropping head first."

"So is everyone else."

Kay couldn't tell who was who in the other green dots on her HUD. Only the commander had that level of detail in their HUD. She did recognize Nassien's unique command beacon and shifted body position until she was moving closer. Her HUD showed her own vitals—pretty calm considering she was screaming head first through the upper atmosphere. Then again, her suit was in full swing, manipulating all her senses and her mood. Wasn't as good as a dose of Prilax, but given it was a sanctioned high, it felt pretty damned good.

The surface remained a dark wasteland. Her HUD detected enemy positions before she had any visuals, but she saw evidence enough of their existence. Anti-aircraft fire shot up in streaks around them.

"The first squads have been detected," Tajex said.

Kay watched two green beacons blink out of existence. Two less soldiers would hit the ground alive.

"Jet's off!" Nassien said.

Kay obeyed. They'd be harder to detect in free-fall. Her HUD showed their slower acceleration from wind shear. Another green dot blinked and disappeared. She checked their time. They had another twenty minutes free-fall before hitting the dirt. That was longer than she wanted to spend at the mercy of some trigger-happy Terran groundsider. She unlocked her rifle and swung it forward.

"What are you doing?" Nassien asked.

"Evening the odds." Kay keyed her HUD into the rifle's targeting scope. The first Terran artillery was just out of her rifle's range. She counted down—three, two, one, and fired. Seconds later, there was one less set of missiles heading their way. She aimed and picked off another Terran position with nuclear bullets. Shooting fish in a barrel was the expression that came to mind after she'd eliminated her third target.

Someone in the Terran camp didn't take kindly to Kay's target practice. Anti-aircraft fire started up with her in the cross hairs. She fired her jets in short bursts, moving in random directions to throw off their targeting. She took out another two targets before Nassien reined her in.

"Rotate and decelerate," Nassien ordered.

Kay reoriented herself so her jets were slowing her down. More Terran fire started up again, but at least there were a few less. They took out more Black March soldiers, but this time, Kay wasn't the only one firing back. Even Nassien unlocked her rifle and picked off targets as they appeared for the next two minutes, until they both had to harness their rifles again and concentrate on hitting the ground.

Kay's HUD brought up enhanced visuals of their landing site. Two burnt-out Terran artillery trenches faced them to the east. Otherwise, the mountainous terrain was covered in a one-meter blanket of snow interrupted only by the blackened marks of artillery explosions.

"Land on your feet," Nassien said. "The suit will absorb the shock. Jets off in three, two, one."

Kay switched off her jets as the ground approached at a pace that still seemed reckless, if not deadly. Trust the suit, that was the mantra right?

She heard the small weapons fire burst before she saw the source. Someone had survived in one of the Terran trenches. She fought the instinct to dive for cover as a bullet pinged off her suit. Nassien didn't. Kay watched her curl away from the sniper right before impacting the ground in a tumbling ball that bounced off rocks and snow for another ten meters before stopping.

"Shit." Kay landed in a crouch, and as soon as she realized she was still in one piece she took two suit-enhanced giant leaps over a deep gully and the rising boulder that separated her from Nassien's position.

Her HUD registered two pings from the Terran sniper, but it wasn't leaving more than a scratch on the suit. Even Nassien's weaker suit was not in any risk.

Nassien straightened out in the snow, then sat up.

"Hell of a landing." Kay crouched next to her. Two other Black March soldiers congregated on their position, Valderrama and one of their other new squad mates.

Nassien's expression took on that distant glaze that said she was scanning her HUD. "The Terrans took their toll. I registered thirteen casualties before landing."

Kay scanned the horizon and her HUD. "Jax?"

"Off the grid, along with Tajex from our squad, and the other three platoons. Terrans must be jamming us."

Kay looked back at Nassien. "You had him until landing, right?"

Nassien checked her display again. "Neither are confirmed casualties. We're out of contact with anyone not in this quadrant. If they drifted to one of the other three attack quadrants, they should be able to join one of the other platoon commanders."

The Terran sniper continued to waste ammo on them as more of their platoon arrived. Nassien turned to one of the latest arrivals. "Take care of that sniper."

The soldier scanned the vicinity, locked on to the sniper's position, and in one leap, landed in the correct trench. There was no more enemy fire.

"One more problem," Nassien said to Kay privately. "My graceless landing took out the actuators in my left leg joints. I think I'm still mobile, but I'll be slowing down the platoon."

"Send them ahead, we'll catch up."

Nassien shook her head. "And who's going to lead them? Tajex is offline, wherever he is. His second in command is dead. Of the ten remaining in our platoon, you are the most mission-knowledgeable."

"Bodyguard, remember? I'm not leaving you here." One plan, she thought. Stay alive. Jax was already beyond her reach. She wasn't letting Nassien go. "Besides, there must be more senior Black March in this platoon."

"Not any more, Corporal."

Corporal? "No. I don't want a field promotion. My place is here, with you."

Nassien leaned forward. "Kay, I need you to lead them. The defense grid isn't on, which means time is critical. This mission has to succeed."

She didn't say it, but Kay heard the words anyway—don't let Halabi win this one. Kay leaned back, and nodded.

Nassien opened a platoon channel. "Platoon commander Tajex is missing, and my suit is in need of repair. Corporal Deetchu is taking command of this mission."

Shit shit shit. Kay eyed up the platoon around her, then made up her mind and stood. "Valderrama."

He stepped around two other platoon mates. His gazed flicked to Nassien in the snow and back to Kay.

"Lieutenant Colonel Nassien's suit is compromised. You'll stay with her while she makes emergency repairs. The rest of the platoon will proceed with the mission." She wanted to order half the platoon to stay behind, but what if one or more were the traitors? Nassien was safest with just Valderrama. He had the firepower to hold off a full Terran platoon so long as no heavy artillery arrived. Kay would make sure none did.

Even through the helmet mask, she saw Valderrama's typical questioning stare. *Is this the mission you screw us, Terran?*

Kay grabbed his mechanized shoulders and jerked him forward until they were mask to mask. "Bring her along at whatever pace she can walk at. Carry her if you have to. You're the only one left I can trust."

He grinned at her. "Hah! I won that bet at least. You are screwing her."

Kay let him go. "Just keep her alive you clanless Novan bastard."

She looked down at Nassien. "Ready." An instant later, her

HUD came alive in command mode. She had a link to the *Aziz* and full tactical and bio readouts for ten green beacons, each with name and rank now. She'd be leaving two of them behind, but not before she pulled up Nassien's readouts and verified the suit only had minor mechanical failure.

"You're stalling." Nassien smiled. "I'm sure you'll leave a nice clean path for us to follow."

"Right." Kay pulled up long-range tactical and scanned the two-kilometer distance that separated them from the gene bank. It was uphill through rocky terrain all the way, with no roads to assist them. She flicked on a broadcast channel. "I've been ordered to take the rest of the platoon forward. The Terrans are entrenched in three waves around the facility, including armored artillery. Speed and armor will only get us part of the way through."

She eyed up the seven soldiers she'd take with her. Two were ex-Marines and the rest were experienced Black March. She pulled two of them to the front with her and split the rest in two groups behind her. "The Terrans know we are here. Their infantry is useless against us but the artillery is deadly. We'll use the natural cover of the terrain to our advantage, but the defense grid is down. That means the gene bank is compromised and if we don't get there fast, they'll destroy it and the mission is a waste. First team goes in fast and targets major artillery. Second and third teams take out the rest. I don't want anything left to come after us."

Or to target Nassien and Valderrama when they followed. She wanted to turn back to Nassien one last time, but that wasn't going to change the situation.

"Go." With armored fists around her rifle, she took off, matched in pace by her two teammates. They leaped over boulders and up the steep slope, leaving a shower of rock and snow for the teams downslope to dodge. The landscape blurred past in a streak of snow and ice and rock. They clocked the first kilometer unopposed. They hit a line of infantry and burst past them without bothering with return fire. The infantry bullets in the first wave were useless. Kay's HUD popped up the more serious long-range Terran targets over the next ridge. That artillery could do real damage.

"First targets coming up. Use the terrain for cover where you can."

With an extra burst, the three of them leaped over the ridge and split wide, to separate the Terrans' targeting options. Artillery fire started the instant they were in range, a range that beat their own rifle-and-rocket-launcher range. The soldier on her right went down in the first volley.

Kay couldn't get a target lock, not with dodging behind cover to keep her hide intact.

They were getting in range for their own rifles. Time for another tactic. "Take them from the sky." With one giant leap, Kay was airborne. The artillery fire didn't track them right away, and she got off two rounds before she landed behind another ridge. Soldiers behind her followed, popping up high to target and destroy with nuclear bullets. It didn't take long to take that artillery site out.

Back on the ground, she scanned her HUD. Two lost. Not bad considering. She pulled up her HUD and studied their perimeter. "The thickest Terran position surrounds the gene bank, outside the mine field. We penetrate that line, and we can track our way through the field."

Her HUD displayed full details of what faced them in the final volley. It wasn't looking good. "There's a full tank division between us and the gene bank. The Terrans must have sky lifted them into position. They aren't mobile, given the terrain, but they have twice the firepower of that last artillery wave."

And how the hell were they going to deal with that? She had five soldiers remaining with her. She brought up details of each. She had one gunner, a sniper, and three regulars. "Spread out in a line. Everyone on nuclear. Gunney, you're in front with me. You hit the field ahead of us with as many nukes as you can launch. The electromagnetic disturbance will force their tank targeting to manual. It will also knock our communications once we start, so get yourselves past this tank line and into the gene bank."

The nuclear confusion wouldn't keep them all alive and they knew it. They were Black March. They formed the line without a word and started a jog uphill. "Gunney, fire in five-second bursts, on my mark."

Kay timed the distance to the tanks. They were nearly in range. "Now!"

The first round exploded in front of them, and they raced through it two seconds later, equally as blind now as the Terrans were. Their line split up into a random pattern to make tracking that much harder. Terran artillery pounded around them, sending clods of debris into the sky. Kay's HUD still displayed all six of them as green and mobile. The gunner shot round after round until the line of tanks were in range.

"Target and fire."

Suit capabilities enhanced with battle stimulants in her system made for a deadly combination for the tank division. She took out the three tanks immediately in front of her and registered multiple more hits from the other Black March soldiers. Six against an armored division, and they were through with only one casualty.

With one final leap, she was in the minefield. Her HUD pulled up the safe track through the field, and she ran with four soldiers at her heels. The field was littered with Terran remains. The Novans obviously weren't the only military willing to toss bodies at a problem. The tactic must have worked, given the lack of defensive response from the gene bank. If she tried, she could likely make out the trail the Terrans used to break into the facility, given the pattern of dead bodies. She didn't try.

It didn't take long for the remaining tanks to start targeting them again. Even with evasive patterns, the tanks needed only to blanket the minefield with artillery. What missed a soldier could hit a mine and have the same net result.

That whole fish in a barrel didn't feel so good when she was the fish.

CHAPTER 14

Gene Study—KDTU-02128 Replicant Status-3077 AH

Crèche G—Replicant R3 deceased—cause of death— accident. Crèche F Replicant 2 (R2) terminated on order of B. Halabi, cause—gene line instability. Complete gene line halt-funding request denied by M. Nassien, XO, overriding Program Manager. M. Nassien analysis— Disregarding the high mortality rate, replicant tactical skills are significantly higher than Terran-normal. Remaining replicant performance to be measured against Marine- based replicants. Classified gene set analysis and reporting to continue outside realm of gene line program manager.

One more green beacon disappeared from Kay's HUD. The fish weren't winning this round. She focused ahead, scanning the rising wall of rock and landslide debris for the bunker hatch. Her HUD tracked it one hundred meters above and to her left. The gunner kept pace at her right. She scanned the cliff face that separated her from the hatch and took one last leap. Her mechanized hands gripped the edge of a protruding rock face as another explosion hit the cliff below her. Too damned close. She swung herself up onto relatively level ground. The hatch was to her right, or really the blast hole where the two meter thick hatch should have been. Looks like some of those Terran bodies made it through.

She pulled her rifle forward. The gunner appeared over the edge ten meters to her right just as another artillery blast hit the cliff between them. The blast took him in the back and propelled him into the relative safety of the blown out bunker entry.

She stepped inside, rifle at the ready, and scanned the area.

Two Terrans fired at her, useless bullets that pinged off her armored suit. She slammed the first into the wall and the body crumpled into a lifeless heap. The second Terran dropped his rifle and surrendered.

Kay ignored him. She pulled up the gunner's stats on her HUD. It showed the injured Black March was one of the ex-Marines, alive, but not functional. She'd have to let the suit's automatic triage take care of him for now.

She turned and squatted in front of the remaining Terran, who backed into the bunker wall, his eyes saucer-wide. "How many inside?" she asked in Terran.

His eyes bulged even more. "Ten."

Not enough to bother them, but plenty to destroy the gene bank if they had enough explosives. "How long ago?"

He eyed Kay's two platoon mates as they scrambled into the bunker entry behind her. "Thirty minutes."

Not a big head start. The Terran could be lying, but seeing how fast he gave up the fight, she doubted it.

Kay picked up the Terran's discarded weapon, a TN70 standard assault rifle, and crushed the tip. She tossed it aside and looked at the two Black March soldiers left to her. Both were experienced Black March. She picked one at random and switched back to Novan. "Stay here, shoot anything Terran that comes in range. If Nassien shows up, you keep her path clear, understood?"

"Yes, ser," she replied with a crisp salute.

She cringed at the soldier's use of the command honorific and scanned the bunker entry. Three more Terran bodies on the floor showed the effectiveness of the bunker's automated internal defenses, but it hadn't been enough. A black, jagged hole showed where the elevator should have been that led down into the bunker. She pulled up a map of the facility on her HUD. It was a thirty-story drop to the first level of the gene bank.

She turned to her remaining platoon mate and pulled his name off her HUD—Syed Kamal, private first class, same as her, or what she used to be before Nassien's field promotions. Assuming Halabi didn't end up in jail, maybe he could get her demoted back after this mission. "Follow me in five."

One step into the black void and she was free falling again. The top of what was left of the elevator raced toward her, the initial pinprick of light resolving into a blast hole the Terrans used to get into the facility. She barely felt the landing as she straddled the hole and scanned the interior. Her HUD picked up nothing within range. She dropped in the hole and stepped into the corridor. Two more Terran dead and one Novan in uniform showed the gene bank security team didn't go down without a fight. Her HUD showed the defense grid control room on this level, with the gene bank cryotanks two levels down.

A thud behind her signaled Kamal's arrival. With only the two of them, and two separate goals, she had limited options. She transmitted her display to his HUD. "Find the cryotanks. If they're secure, keep them that way. If they aren't, make them secure."

Kamal hesitated a moment as he scanned the new data in his HUD, then took off to the left, skipping over one of the Terran dead tangled with the Novan security officer.

Kay took off in the opposite direction. Drab tan paint covered smoothed rock walls and cement flooring. Only the ceiling showed any differentiation, with a constant array of security cameras and targeting weapons, all inoperable. The fact that ten Terrans could take out the internal security showed how much faith the Novans had in their external security and minefield. That overconfidence might just have cost them this gene bank.

"Never underestimate the power of a few grunts," she muttered as she made her way down the corridor.

Her HUD picked up three live beacons ahead, one Novan, two Terrans. She locked her rifle in place across her back and switched to her hand pistol and enhanced her audio feed.

"How much longer?" the first Terran asked, male voice.

"If you could get that damned Novan to talk, this would be easier," a second voice, possibly female, said from further away. "I'm guessing where the critical parts are to this defense grid equipment. I've got another four explosives to arm."

Kay needed some subtlety if she wanted to keep that Novan alive. She pulled out a remote camera bot, the size of a marble, and let it loose. It engaged with her HUD instantly, and she maneuvered it into the opened doorway just ahead. One Terran guarded a Novan tech sporting a minor head wound. The other Terran was out of range, likely strapping explosives to the equipment.

Kay stepped through the open doors to the defense grid control room. The first Terran swung around to face her. Two bullets pinged off her suit.

"Do I look like target practice?" She crushed his windpipe in her metal grip as she scanned the rest of the room for the last Terran.

He emerged from the racks of equipment to her left and got off a round well wide of her before she blasted a hole in his chest. It wasn't until she heard the groan that she realized who the real target was. The Novan tech slumped across the control panel, blood already spilling to the floor.

Shit. She needed that technician alive.

She pulled the tech to the floor. Her HUD showed diminishing vitals that disappeared before she even started to strip her mechanized gloves off. So much for using local talent to fire up the defense grid. She leaned back on her knees and keyed her comm to the Black March soldier guarding the entrance. "Any sign of Nassien?"

"No, ser."

Ser. Authority sucked.

"The Terrans are landing more artillery, though. Looks like a full-armored division. And they're sending troops into the mine field."

Nassien wouldn't make it through that Terran line. "Are the Terrans hitting any mines?"

"No, ser."

"They mapped our safe trail through the field. Keep them at bay as long as you can, then get down to the cryotanks."

Kay switched to Kamal's link. "Any activity?"

"Five Terrans eliminated. The cryotanks are rigged with explosives, but no detonators yet."

"Okay, I'm sending you some help. We have incoming enemy troops. Keep that area secure."

Kay scanned the control room. She didn't have a whole lot of options in front of her. She locked her gloves back on and started with sealing the door and barricading it with anything that wasn't strapped down. It wouldn't keep anyone out for long, but they were all dead anyway if she couldn't stop the Terran advance.

She pushed the tech's body to the side and stared down at the control panel. It looked just like the simulator, but it wouldn't act like it. She unlocked and removed her gloves again as she studied the controls. She recognized the external feeds and pulled them onscreen first. Artillery fire went off toward and away from the bunker entry. Nassien and Valderrama must be keeping them busy. The line of Terran dead bodies showed Kamal was still in control up above, but wouldn't stay that way for long.

She looked back down at the controls. Nassien's confidence that no Terran would dare connect to the grid came back to haunt her. She had two choices—fire up the grid and see how long she could last before her brain fried, or wait like sitting ducks until the Terrans overran the place.

Dead if you do and dead if you don't.

Kay pulled off her helmet and dropped it into the chair she couldn't use in her suit anyway. She pulled on a slim pair of gloves linked wirelessly into the grid controls. Now or never. With a flick of her wrist, she booted the system and watched the status messages fly by on the flat screen. Everything came up green, functional.

The skullcap sat beside the flat screen. It didn't look like much, but in Kay's experience, it didn't take much to fry a few brain cells. She stretched it over her head and pulled down the visor that would block out any distractions.

Her mouth felt dry. This was not going to be good, not good at all. She flipped the connect switch with one finger and her world changed in an instant. Targeting data slammed into her brain from a hundred sensor and firing options that made up the defense grid. She shut her eyes on instinct, but it didn't lessen the needles of pain shooting through her head.

Breathe. Just breathe.

It didn't stop the flood of data, but gave her just enough sanity to get beyond the pain and focus on what she learned from watching Nassien's practice runs. Pick a target and eliminate it. She flexed each finger to track which firing option it defaulted to, but even that proved too much to follow over the pain. She had to trust the system would mark and avoid any friendlies in the target area.

Jaws clenched, she twitched her thumb and forefinger on each hand. Two semiautomatics spread fire across the center of the minefield, followed a split second later by explosions just in front of the line of Terran artillery. She twitched thumbs again and was rewarded with one destroyed tank. Thumbs equal missile launchers. Good to know.

Four fingers on each hand twitched, taking out a random number of Terran infantry who had followed her path through the minefield. She focused what little brainpower she had on the thumb targets. Tanks and artillery bad. Thumbs kill. It was the simplest mantra, maybe simple enough to keep her sanity through the splitting headache already pounding through her overworked brain. She fired.

And fired. And fired again.

Reflex took over where her conscious brain couldn't function. The grid pulled as much out of her as she could give and then some. Where she twitched, explosions flared. It was ten, a hundred times faster than the shipboard simulation.

Target acquisition and elimination, left hand, right hand. Independent and simultaneous.

Her vision blurred. She'd stopped blinking. Forcing a conscious thought to take care of that activity cut her off from the next round of targets. Disorientation took over. She was losing control of the grid. Elements fired without her command. Was she hitting friendlies or enemies? Her brain screamed pull out!

CHAPTER 15

Gene Study—KDTU-02128 Replicant Status-3079 AH

Stage 4, Crèche F—Three replicants survived first two years active duty in Marines. Two remain active. One deserted. Biometric tracking found and terminated the replicant, on order of Program Manager B. Halabi. Full psych analysis ordered across the gene line, with priority 1 reports sent directly to M. Nassien. All replicant early termination orders halted until analysis completed.

Pain. Twitching fingers and thumbs. Little else existed in Kay's small world. A faint thought registered that she'd lost control, but it was crowded out by tactical data—target acquisition, target destroyed. She made a good solid hole in the Terran artillery line, she remembered that much.

The display popped up the friendly beacons of more Black March soldiers. She couldn't see who or where through the internal haze of target and fire, target and fire.

Background noise filtered through, banging. Explosions inside the facility? If she had any self-preservation left, she'd disengage. Her fingers continued twitching her assault on the Terrans. Slowly, the blinding pain in her head lessened. Her fingers and thumbs continued to twitch of their own accord until logic told her that her actions weren't coinciding with anything that happened in the grid anymore. Rapid-fire precision hits across the Terran front line replaced her erratic firing pattern. She knew the cause before she managed to pull her gloves and skullcap off to see for herself.

Valderrama stood guard at the blackened remnants of a

doorway. That was what she'd heard, when they blew apart her makeshift barricade. So much for being able to react to that early warning when she was locked into the defense grid. She'd be dead now if it had been Terrans breaking into the compromised control room.

Nassien had managed to fold herself into the control seat and wore the secondary skullcap and gloves. "What part of 'dangerous to Terrans' didn't you understand?"

She could talk and control the grid? Kay lowered herself to the floor and rested her head in her hands. Terran genes sucked. "The part where a Terran V-5 artillery line landed in between me and you." She fought back the urge to vomit. "Anything in this suit's magic pharmacy for splitting headaches?"

Nassien's fingertips moved with smooth precision, something Kay was sure hers hadn't. "Put your helmet back on and trigger a med cycle."

Kay picked up her helmet and paused. "What's that going to do to my situational readiness?"

"As if you are in any way fit for active duty right now?" Nassien quirked a smile. "Put it on and check your HUD."

Kay locked her helmet on and fired up the HUD. Still in command mode, she watched green dots sprinkle the display, including one important one. "Jax is here."

"Yes, and a good half of a platoon with them. The site is secure."

Secure. She was alive, Nassien and Jax were alive. Mission accomplished. "Med cycle engaged."

Command mode on her HUD switched back to Nassien. Her HUD display went from external to internal sensors. A stream of medical data scrolled by, ending with a prognosis and triage plan that meant nothing to her except for a five-minute timer it left in the upper right corner. That's how long the suit would keep her immobile while filling her with drugs. She felt the tiny prick of a needle in her shoulder and another in her neck. Her headache dampened seconds later, as the countdown continued. She could see Nassien busy at the grid, and Valderrama leaning against the blasted doorframe. Drowsiness took over a moment later, and she closed her eyes.

It felt like seconds later that Kay heard a large thump. She forced her sleepy eyes open. Valderrama was slumped in the doorway, as immobile as she was. It was a sight she'd seen before.

She struggled against inertia and flicked on a private channel to Nassien. "Valderrama's down!" Her HUD countdown said two minutes, thirteen seconds.

Nassien disengaged from the defense grid. She turned in her seat just as Jax and Tajex rushed through the blackened doorway. Kay's timer ticked down. Jax ran to Kay. She was too lethargic from the drugs to force another comm channel change, but she saw her sense of relief reflected in his eyes.

That relief died the instant she saw Tajex lift his rifle. Reality slammed through her drug-addled brain. "Dive!"

Nassien reacted but Tajex was faster. Two bullets blasted through Nassien's armor, one in the shoulder, and the other in the chest. Jax scrambled to his feet as Nassien slumped to the floor, landing across Kay's immobile form.

Kay stared into eyes slowly losing focus. "No," she whispered.

Nassien's hand reached for hers, covered from view by Nassien's ineffective armored suit. "Engaging med cycle." Her eyes shut.

Kay looked back up. Two minutes, five seconds. Jax stood in front of her. "Kay comes with me."

Tajex lowered his rifle. "We've got five minutes to arm the charges and get out of here."

"I'll carry her then."

Tajex tossed him an explosive detonator from the stash the Terrans were working from. "If she talks when we turn her suit back on, she's dead."

Jax caught the detonator. "She won't talk."

She won't talk, but you'll be just as dead, Tajex. Kay held onto Nassien's hand. Countdown, one minute, forty seconds.

Time moved at a Prilax-like crawl, every second ticking, as she wondered if Nassien's suit was good enough to keep her alive, while Kay could only stare at the final two traitors. How many deaths were on Tajex hands? Worse than that, how many had Jax helped on?

Forty-five seconds. A tear streamed down her cheek but she had no way to wipe it away. His betrayal burned through her as she watched Jax strap his rifle into place across his back and pick up another charge detonator. He and Tajex disappeared into the equipment racks.

Thirty seconds. Another set of needles pierced her skin. Her head tingled, and then adrenaline flowed to her system. She was wide awake and knew exactly what she would do.

"I've got the last detonator," Tajex said from somewhere in the racks. "Collect that body bag if you're taking her with us."

Fully engaged and back in command mode now, Kay sought out Jax's green dot and sent him the same system reboot command he used on Valderrama. Jax walked out of the equipment rack. She didn't think they'd leave themselves vulnerable to that trick.

He came and squatted in front of her and stripped her of rifle, grenade launcher, and machine gun. "I'll reengage your suit as soon as we clear the bunker." He turned to Nassien. "Sorry about her. Guess you won't miss Valderrama, though, eh?"

Thanks for the reminder. Kay sought out the grey dot that was Valderrama and triggered a suit reboot. In five-and-a-half minutes, he'd be up and ready to blow a hole through any survivors. She kept herself immobile while Jax hoisted her up and over his shoulder so her head and arms dangled down his back. He turned to face the doorway, blocking her view of the racks.

She switched her HUD to his display. Tajex came into view, his rifle still in hand as he turned back to eye up his handiwork. It was the point of maximum vulnerability for them and the time to act.

Kay unsnapped Jax's rifle underneath her and gave one quick burst to her left boot jets. She flew sideways off his shoulder, rolled, and fired. The bullet blasted through Tajex helmeted head just has he was turning back to face them.

"Damn it, Kay!" Jax stood two paces from her, his pistol aimed at her head.

Kay dropped the rifle. "Are you really going to kill me now?" She stood, very slowly, keeping her hand away from her harnessed pistol.

Jax kept the pistol pointed at her but lowered his arm. "Shit. Now you've got to act like the hero? We would have been free, all three of us."

"Free from what? We'd be fugitives. Or were you planning on joining the Terrans?" The look on Jax's face told her that was exactly what they'd planned.

He glanced at Tajex. "Why did you have to kill him? He was my family."

"There was a time we were family."

"Then you let her in." He waved his gun at Nassien's prone form.

"And you let him in." Time wasn't on Kay's side. Disarm or eliminate, those were her options. Jax had even less, since Valderrama was witnessing this all, even if he couldn't move yet. Whatever his plans were, she killed them when she killed Tajex and powered up Valderrama.

"We're still family," she said. "And family takes care of each other."

Kay raised her right hand to him. One mission goal, to take care of herself, Nassien, and Jax. Her eyes met his reddish-brown eyes. He lowered his pistol.

She fired Nassien's blade out of her powered wrist sheath. It sliced through Jax's chest armor and left only the ornate hilt exposed. Jax slumped to the ground, his confused brain losing control of the suit's actions.

Kay crouched down next to him. "My HUD shows fifteen more Black March in and around the facility, and Valderrama's thirty seconds from active. You'd have been caught and tortured as a traitor."

"They don't have a right to own us like this. You know that." His glassy eyes stared at her. "Kay, I'm sorry."

"Me, too." She watched his yellow beacon in her HUD turn black, one more casualty. She shut her eyes against the pain, with no way to brush away the tears.

"Are they both dead?" Valderrama asked, moments later.

Nassien. Kay pulled up her stats on her HUD. "She's alive, barely." She keyed in a com link to the *Aziz*. "This is Corporal Deetchu, acting officer-in-charge. We need an emergency med evac at the gene bank bunker."

"Acknowledged. Rubicon's drones are spread out in the airspace around you," an unrecognizable comm officer responded. "There's no option to land at this point."

"Lieutenant Colonel Nassien is down. She needs evac immediately."

"Understood, Corporal, but unless you can clear the airspace, we have no way of retrieving her."

Shit. Kay looked at the defense grid. "I'll make a window. Get that evac team ready."

She signed off and scanned the tactical positions of the fifteen Black March troops. A third were inside the facility, the rest holding back the Terran Infantry. That would keep her back door safe, now she just needed to open the front door above, for the *Aziz*.

"Valderrama, keep that door secure. No one comes in except the med evac team, understood?"

"Yes, ser." He positioned himself at the burned-out entry, rifle loaded and ready.

She pulled off her helmet and dropped it to the floor next to Nassien's unconscious body. *Stay alive, damn it.*

Her skullcap and gloves lay where she had left them. She pulled them on, ignoring the spattering of Nassien's blood on them and the control panel. She took a deep breath, and then reintegrated herself into the defense grid.

Her headache returned the instant the grid recognized a new controller. So much for that med cycle healing her. She tried to block out all the surface targets that the Black March could cover. Shifting her focus to the sky was the easy part. The sheer number of drones darting in and out of her targeting options was insane. She twitched her fingers and ignited a burst of fire, but hit nothing. Shit. Focus. It was her against some faceless Terran tac officer.

A part of her was fighting the grid, rather than working with it, but that felt like self-preservation. It wasn't going to open a space for the med evac team, though. With a last, shallow breath, she let go.

Her headache got worse as the grid took control of her. Clenching her jaw against the pain, she scanned the airspace above the bunker. The grid locked onto a target. She felt a tiny jolt on a finger and twitched. Anti-aircraft missile launched and destroyed one drone. Another lock, another twitch. She was working in harmony with the grid controls for once, targets locking and disappearing faster and faster. The grid took whatever she could give, and then some. She couldn't tell if her fingers were twitching in reaction to the grid requests or if she was getting muscle spasms, it all came so fast.

Pain stabbed through her head like a hot knife, but the grid kept going, sending signals to both hands. She could barely sense her right hand, but the left kept twitching, eliminating targets.

The sky space was clearing as her vision narrowed to a dark tunnel, and then, nothing.

CHAPTER 16

Gene Study—KDTU-02128 Replicant Status-3080 AH

Stage 4 Status—One replicant remains. Program Manager B. Halabi resigned, with gene line management temporarily reporting directly to M. Nassien. Classified gene set analysis ended on Crèche F. Stage 5 experimental records sealed per order of M. Nassien.

Suffocation. *Breathe, Kay, Breathe.* Her mind couldn't control her lungs. Then, a breath. Forced.

"She's got movement on her left side only." An unknown voice.

"Can she hear me?" A known voice. Kay wanted to hear that one, but silence swallowed her again.

She was in a dark tunnel. Where was Jax? Something followed her, a scratching, feral animal sound echoed off the dank tunnel walls. She had to escape that animal or die. Water splashed up her bare feet as she ran. The tunnel turned ahead. She came to a sudden stop. Don't go there.

Ahead or back, death waited for her either way. The animal sounds came closer. Fear pushed her forward. She rounded the corner and fell to her knees in the cold water. Nassien leaned against the tunnel wall, her lifeblood leaking from a knife wound, brown eyes going lifeless as Kay watched. Jax lay across her, with the same wound, leaking his orange-red blood in a steady flow. Kay clutched the knife in her bloody hands. A scream built in her lungs.

Silence.

"Was a success."

Warm hands enveloped hers. The voice, again, but the matching name wouldn't come to her.

"Two weeks out from New China. We've got the best regen facilities there."

A hand moved to stroke her hair. "The captain of the *Aziz* put us both in for promotions. Sorry, I guess I told you that before, though. Huda tells me I should talk about more interesting things."

Kay struggled against it, but the silence crept in again and the voice faded away anyway.

Breaths came more easily, a slow steady rhythm that Kay controlled. She relaxed into it. She cracked open resistant eyes to a blurry light she tried to blink into focus. There was face to her left, where someone held her hand. She blinked, again. Nassien, alive. Her hand tightened instinctively.

"I felt that!" Nassien turned away. "Nurse, tell the doctor she's more responsive today."

Kay opened her mouth, but all that escaped was a dry rasp.

A tear trailed down Nassien's cheek. "It's okay. I know you're here this time. You've had your eyes open for days, but the doctor said that's normal when a patient comes out of a forced coma."

Coma? Kay turned her head, but something uncomfortable tugged at her nose. She recognized it as an oxygen line. She tried to speak again, to ask what happened, but her voice wasn't obeying.

"Try this." Nassien held a cup and straw up to Kay's lips. She took a slow sip, then another.

"What," she rasped.

Nassien didn't answer. Instead, she leaned over and kissed her. Kay shut her eyes and sleep took over.

Kay woke up later, screaming. "Nassien's down. Jax is down!"

She fought against the faceless bodies restrained her. She recognized the drug-induced lethargy that took control a moment later.

She didn't know how much later she opened her eyes. Nassien and Huda watched over her, one on the left, the other the right.

"You're safe, now. The doctor explained some coma patients experience an episode of ICU psychosis. You'll be fine," Nassien said, but the worried expression on her face told a different story.

Kay nodded. Nassien was alive. It was only nightmares. Drugs could do that sometimes.

"Explain to her again, Ayaan," Huda said. "She probably doesn't remember."

Nassien held Kay's hand. "We transferred from the *Aziz* to a hospital ship with the rest of the wounded. You've been in an induced coma for three weeks. The doctor's say your recovery is going well."

Recovery from what? Crap, why couldn't she remember? She shook her head, but it still felt like lead. It didn't matter though, she was alive, and Nassien was alive. One more to check off.

"Jax?" she said, in a whisper. She was facing Nassien, but she sensed Huda move on her left.

"You should rest," Huda said. "The doctor will limit visitation time if we tire you out, dear."

A nurse appeared, causing Nassien to shift to the side. Kay recognized that drill. "No. Drugs."

The nurse shook his head. "You need rest."

Kay turned to Nassien. "Nightmares." Her expression must have relayed her fears.

Nassien put a restraining hand on the nurse. "No drugs."

"Ser, it's the doctor's recommendation that KDTU—"

"Her name is Kay, and you said yourself it is a recommendation, not a requirement. No drugs," Nassien said in a voice that expected obedience. The nurse backed off.

"No more questions, though," Huda said, with a glance at Nassien. "You do need rest."

It was the last thing she wanted, but with Huda gone, and Nassien sitting at her side, sleep overtook her anyway.

The next time she woke up, she was alone, and she remembered. Silent tears streamed down her cheeks, and she couldn't even lift her right hand to wipe them off, something else they were keeping from her. She stewed in silence, ignoring the quiet beeps of the equipment surrounding her. The hospital ship was significantly better equipped than any other shipboard medical facility she'd ever been on. Then again, she'd never been injured bad enough to require a stay on a hospital ship. Her compartment was spartan, one bed, equipment, and a side chair. She owed that solo status to Nassien for sure. A low-ranking rat like her would normally be in a suite of four at least, if not bunked up to eight.

A nurse entered the compartment, and the muted lighting kicked in. Kay didn't recognize her and couldn't be bothered taxing her weakened memory to try. "What's wrong with my arm?"

The nurse checked the equipment surrounding Kay first, and then gave her an empty smile. "Glad to see you awake. Are you hungry?"

Kay stomach grumbled in answer but she ignored it. "My right arm. I can't control it."

"That's for the doctor to discuss."

"Then get the doctor. Now," Kay said in her best command voice.

It came out more like the rasp of an alcoholic in the dredges of a bad hangover, but maybe it worked. The nurse disappeared, and Kay waited. When the hatch opened, she expected someone in the white medic's uniform. Nassien stepped in instead, in black fatigues. The smile she gave Kay barely touched her sad eyes. This was not going to be good.

"My arm?" she asked.

Nassien sat on her left side, and now Kay understood why as Nassien held the one functional hand she had. "Partial paralysis on your right extremities, arm, and leg."

At least she didn't try to cushion it. Kay couldn't take the sad sympathy in those brown eyes. She turned to the ceiling and fought the return of tears.

Nassien held her face in a warm hand and turned her back.

"It's temporary. We're three days out from New China, with the best nerve regeneration facility. I've been in communications, and they are waiting for us."

Kay couldn't stop the tear that spilled, but Nassien wiped it away. She closed her eyes. It was too much to take in. Jax had been her lifeline for so many years, and she'd killed him. Her body was only partially functional. What the hell was her future now?

She opened her eyes. "What happens after that, Ma'am?"

Nassien caressed her cheek. "Ayaan, please."

"You're my commanding officer."

"Until we get to New China. I'm retiring after this mission, and so are you."

Kay couldn't help the sarcasm that edged her raspy voice. "Gene lines only have one retirement plan, the Black March. I'm already there."

"That I will deal with as well," Nassien said in a hardened voice. She took a deep breath. "What do you want, when you've recovered?" she asked, her voice softer.

"I'm still your bodyguard. Huda said that's a permanent job."

Nassien shook her head. "You didn't answer my question. What is it that you want?"

Nobody asked a gene line what they wanted. Their lives were controlled from crèche to grave. Kay took in Nassien's question, her vulnerability, and her fear. She lifted Nassien's hand from her cheek and held it in hers. "I want what keeps me with you."

Nassien leaned in to rest her head on Kay's. "I think I can arrange that."

"I should hope so. What's the point of having an uber-powerful girlfriend if she can't pull a few strings now and then."

That earned her both a smile and a slap. She kissed that smile, and let herself believe that maybe they would be all right in the end.

After all, her right arm had felt the sting of that slap.

ABOUT THE AUTHOR

This is where an author would normally include her biography. In place of that, Sandra included the following four tidbits about herself. Three are flat-out lies, one is a true:

- She was arrested as a teenager, but her police officer uncle got her off with a warning.

- She is terrified of balloons. Terrified.

- Spiders on the other hand, are a-okay after she ate one on a dare in the sixth grade.

- She paddles her kayak in the sheep pasture when it floods.

Email her at sbarret_fic@yahoo.com with your guess on which one is true, or visit her website at http://www.sandrabarret.com for a more traditional bio.